HEAD IN THE GAME

Lily Cahill

This is a work of fiction. Names, characters, places, and incidents either are the product of the author's imagination, or are used fictitiously. Any resemblance to actual persons, living or dead, events, or locales, are entirely coincidental.

Copyright © 2016 Nameless Shameless Women, LLC.

All rights reserved.

CHAPTER ONE
Lilah

"There is absolutely nothing in my wardrobe that says 'college professor.'"

My grandmother glances over to where I stand in the kitchen doorway, wearing two different shoes, a bell skirt, and a bra. "Why don't you go like that?" she says dryly. "You'll certainly make an impression."

I am not in the mood for humor. "Gamma, what was I thinking? I can't teach a college class."

"And why not?" she says with an arch of her eyebrow. She pulls a bowl out of the cabinet and fills it with granola.

"I never should have agreed to this," I say, flopping down in one of the chairs in my ridiculous half-outfit. "Did I tell you? When Marty first asked me to take over his classes for the summer session, I laughed in his face. I should have stuck with my initial instincts. This is a terrible idea."

"Oh, hush," Gamma says as she pulls berries and milk out of the fridge and adds them to the bowl. "Eat this, and I'll fix your hair. You are going to be a wonderful professor."

Head in the Game

"I am basically the same age as all of the students," I say, snatching up the bowl. I'm not the kind of girl who lets anxiety affect my appetite.

"But far more experienced," Gamma points out as she slips behind me and gathers up my hair. "Did you or did you not start painting landscapes before you could talk?"

"All babies finger paint," I point out through a mouthful of granola, then wince as Gamma tugs on a strand of the loose braid she's weaving down the top of my head. I recently shaved the sides of my head on a whim, leaving me with a mohawk of thick, black hair.

"You started winning contests when you were ten," my grandmother points out. "And started selling paintings before you were in high school. God knows, that money has helped us through some tough times."

"I don't mind," I tell my grandmother for the thousandth time, and though I can't see her, I know she's shaking her head.

In my artist's eye, I can see the way we look together. We're both big women, tall and curvy, with the same mahogany skin. Gamma wears a crisp, white blouse with pink piping, a matching pink sweater, and a small gold cross necklace. Her hair is shaped into the same gray ball that has surrounded her face since I was born. I, on the other hand, am wearing a combat boot on one foot and a spiked heel on the other. Colorful tattoos spin up one arm and across my chest, where my sizable breasts are displayed in a zebra-print bra. And my grandmother is putting the finishing touches on my two-inch-high mohawk.

It would make a good portrait, I muse. If I did that

kind of thing.

"I'm both ashamed and proud to say that you've had enough success over the years to support us both," my grandmother says. "But I still wish you could have gone to art school."

I reach up to touch her hand, so familiar within my own. "I didn't *want* to go to art school." That isn't true, and we both know it. Still, I try to put a good face on it. "Fifty grand to learn stuff I can find on the Internet? Not worth it."

"I know full well you stayed home because of my heart," my grandmother says as she ties the last strands of my braid into place. "It's been three years since my heart attack. When are you going to stop worrying?"

As if that's an option. I had come home from school when I was seventeen and found my grandmother collapsed, barely breathing, surrounded by the bags of groceries she'd been carrying into the house. I'd almost lost her, and I've worried about her every day since.

"You're a good girl, Lilah," Gamma continues when I don't answer. "You're going to knock the socks off those college kids. I bet none of them have won the Pitkin Prize."

I squirm a bit. "I bet none of those college kids have even heard of the Pitkin Prize."

"Well, then they're ignorant, and you should tell them all about it," she says. "Lilah, you won one of the most prestigious contests in the nation. You have a painting on display in the MOMA. If you aren't going to brag about it, I'll just have to do it for you."

Just to prove her point, she pulls her phone out of her pocket.

"Don't you dare," I burst out as she busily works the screen.

"You think I'm not going to tell my friends that my baby is teaching a college class? I'm proud as a peacock."

That warms my heart and eases my nerves. "All right, fine. But don't mention the Pitkin."

"Why not?" she asks absently, busy composing the perfect humble-brag.

"I don't know." On the table, I sketch mountains with the tip of my finger. "It feels like bragging."

"It's not bragging if I do it for you. And why shouldn't you be proud of yourself?"

"I am." That sounds like a lie, even to me. I repeat the words, making some effort to sound like I mean it. "I am proud. It's just ... with everything that's happened ... I wish I had never gone to New York to accept the prize."

My grandmother lays her hand on my shoulder. "You know it's not your fault. What happened to Natalie."

A river of hot emotion runs through me at the sound of Natalie's name. I nod as I attempt to swallow the flood back down. "I know it in my head. It's my heart that isn't so sure."

"I know all about regret, my girl." Gamma presses her lips together. I know she's thinking about my mother, because her eyes turn heavy and sad. "But you can't change the past. All you can do is learn from it, and take your joys where you can."

I take a deep breath. I'm perilously close to crying, and that would be a terrible way to start any day. But it's especially terrible today, when I need to feel confident and strong. I manage a smile for my grandmother. "Okay. You're right. Brag about me all you want."

Gamma lights up. "That's my girl. Now, go put on that pink crop top I like and your leopard print shoes. That gold skirt will be just fine. And," she says, shimmying her shoulders at me, "after you've done your makeup, we are taking a selfie."

Gamma has embraced social media to an astonishing degree. I think she has more Instagram followers than me.

"All right," I say with mock-exasperation. "But I get to pick the filter. After all, I'm the artist."

"That's my girl."

I loose one final sigh, letting my shoulders sag. "Are you sure I can do this?"

Gamma lay her hands on my cheeks, her eyes filled with love and pride. "Lilah, I'm certain you can do anything."

I try to hang on to those words on my way to the campus of Mountain State University. It is a glorious morning. Sun showers down on me from a brilliant blue sky as I ride my bike along the river trail cutting through the town center. The water is running high now at the beginning of summer, and I spy a group of college-aged guys paddling their way through the current atop a couple of huge inner tubes.

It's hard not to feel happy when you live in a beautiful place. Even with all the horrible stuff that has happened in the last six months, I still love living in Granite, Colorado.

I grew up here, hiking in the surrounding mountains and hanging out with the artsy kids on the Diamond Street pedestrian mall. The town built a reputation for hippies and liberal politics in the 1960s. But in the past twenty years, since Coach Moe Foster came to town, we've had a reputation for something else—football.

The MSU Mustangs are one of the best teams in the nation. Or, they were. Before all the shit that went down at the end of last year's season. A lot of people say they don't deserve the punishment they got. I say, a lot of people are wrong.

Someone who cares could give you statistics, but all I know is that every year, for my entire life, college football has been the most important thing in this town. And it still is, but the definition of "important" has changed. It had been something of which we were proud. But then it became the source of the biggest scandal in the university's—and our town's—history.

The river path rises up and I suddenly find myself there—on the MSU campus. I've barely been here since Thanksgiving, when Natalie and I came to check out the student film festival. A month after that, I had been in New York accepting the Pitkin, and Natalie had come here to a party. Alone.

The campus is stately, manicured, and relatively empty since most of the students are gone for summer break. In the distance, I can just see the stadium peeking out from between the golden-pink sandstone buildings.

Without warning, a wave of anger washes over me. So hot, I have to stop my bike. I've never been a fan of football, but growing up, there was no way to avoid it. It was a condition of living in Granite, like snow in the winter. It used to just be an annoyance—not being able to get around on Saturdays due to the tailgates and drunken fans, listening to a persistent buzz about a topic I cared nothing about, struggling to find something else to do during games since every other single person in Granite was glued to the game. Now, everything about football fills me with rage.

I take a deep breath to settle my nerves. I still can't believe I've agreed to teach Introduction to Art for the summer session while Marty Carlson is on sabbatical. But he caught me at a weak moment, when I had been trying (by which I mean failing) to paint for over an hour. Ever since the Pitkin, I've been creatively blocked. I'm becoming a cliché—the artist who can't handle her own success.

Marty is a good guy. He's been selling my paintings in his gallery for nearly a decade. I don't think I was his first choice to take over while he went back East to help his sick mother, but I'd been the first one to say yes. Which, I've come to think, was a terrible idea. I know plenty about painting, but I've never had to teach anyone else. And this class covers pottery and line drawing as well. It's only the first day, and I already feel like I'm in over my head.

I'm hoping that getting back to the basics will unlock something inside me. Maybe teaching others will help me see where I've lost my center. Or maybe it will just keep my mind occupied while my subconscious works through the block.

Plus, the money won't hurt. I have other sources of income, but Gamma's heart medicine costs a fortune. If I don't start selling paintings soon, I'll have to dip into the nest egg that I've worked so hard to build.

I agreed to do this. I have to at least give it a shot.

The art building is easy enough to find, but it doesn't stop my heart from thudding with anxiety. I

Head in the Game

haven't even been inside the classroom yet. And I'm supposed to be the professor? It feels like some sort of joke. A professor who hasn't even earned a college degree.

But there's no going back now—not after how proud Gamma is of me. After a pause, I open the door, and all my apprehensions wash away in a flood of pure pleasure.

The classroom is an atrium, the north wall made entirely of windows. Beyond the glass lies a breathtaking view of the Rocky Mountains cradling a clear sky. The room smells faintly of canvas and turpentine, and the wood floor is speckled with years of paint. If I had dreamed of a classroom, it would look exactly like this.

I wander the room, familiarizing myself with the supplies. For this first class, I was planning on covering the basics of watercolors and oils, so I'm pleased to see that some graduate student has stocked the storage shelves with everything I need.

Maybe this won't be so bad. I'm already thinking about ways to adjust my prepared lectures. They're all too formal, too stiff. A room like this is full of distractions, and I can use that. The easels and tables are on casters, which will make it simple to use all the different spaces in the room. What if I ask the students to spend a few minutes each day mixing a color the exact same blue as the sky?

Behind me, the classroom door clicks open. I turn, expecting to see that the department head has come to greet me.

The man currently filling the doorway definitely isn't the dainty, effete department head. This guy is tall, broad, and heavily muscled. And, some part of me adds, mouth-wateringly sexy. His strong jaw is clean-shaven, and his honey-colored hair is still wet from a recent shower. I feel a purely female pulse echo through me as my mouth goes dry.

Then I notice the silver Mustangs logo on his blue T-shirt and the workout bag slung over his shoulder emblazoned with MSU Football. Dammit. He's a football player.

"Are you lost?" I say, my words harder than usual.

"I don't think so," he says, in a voice that holds the cadence of wide open spaces. "I'm pretty sure I'm looking for you."

CHAPTER TWO
Riley

"I mean, I'm looking for this *class*. Intro to Art, right?" I say quickly, trying to cover my mistake. But the truth is, I feel the same way looking at this woman as I do right after I've taken a hard hit. Both things are in danger of taking me straight to the ground.

She is stunning. Sexy and edgy and soft-bodied, like a wet dream of curves and moldable flesh. She is all color and pattern, dark skin and wild hair and bold makeup. I don't know where to look, can't stop myself from dragging my eyes all the way down her body and back up again.

Right back to her gorgeous … *angry* face.

"I'm Riley Brulotte," I say, flashing a smile. "Are you a student in this class?"

"I'm the teacher in this class," she says, her eyebrow arched.

Wait. What? I pull out my phone and find my class schedule with a couple of clicks. "So you're Professor Martin Carlson?"

She frowns and steps closer to me. "They must not have updated the schedule. Marty had to go out of town suddenly, and he asked if I would take over the class. I'm Lilah Stone."

She's wearing perfume, something spicy and hot that makes me wonder how it would taste on her skin. This woman isn't afraid to make an impact. And she's certainly having an effect on me.

I hold out my hand to shake, eager to discover if her skin is as soft as I imagine. "Nice to meet you, Ms. Stone."

She frowns again at that. "Not Ms. Stone. That's way too weird. I hadn't really thought about … well. You should probably call me Lilah."

"Lilah," I say. Damn, that's a sexy name. It fits her perfectly. "It's a pleasure."

She stares up at me for a moment, her lips parted, her hand in mine. Something flickers in her eyes before she takes back her hand and sticks it in the pocket of her skirt. "Well. Uh … what did you say your name was?"

"Riley." I have to be honest: It's kind of nice not being recognized. I'm the starting tight end for the Mustangs, and I've had sportscasters and NFL scouts talking about me for years. They've even given me a nickname—"Lotto" Brulotte. Hell, the fans call it "winning the lottery" when I take down the opposing defense. In this little world, I'm famous. But this woman clearly has no idea who I am. It's, well, refreshing.

"Well, Riley," Lilah says, "you have your pick of seats." She leaves me standing in the doorway and busies herself behind the desk, pulling papers and a laptop from her big leather bag. "Class will start in just a few minutes."

I drop my backpack and gym bag next to a chair

and am about to collapse into it—it was a long practice earlier—but something stops me. I don't want this conversation with Lilah to be over yet. I wander closer to her and say, "I'm looking forward to this class."

She makes a little huffing sound of disbelief.

"What?"

She looks me up and down. "You're a football player, right?"

"Yes, ma'am. Tight end. Have you ever gone to an MSU game?"

She shakes her head, but it seems more in disbelief than an answer to my question. "Look, maybe Marty ran this class for an easy A, but that's not how I'm going to do it."

Irritation prickles at me. "I don't need an easy A."

"Then what are you doing here?"

"Taking an art class?" I keep my voice steady despite the growing indignation at what she's implying. "I've always wanted to."

She cocks her head. "What, like, to meet girls?"

I'm not one for fancy pick-up lines. Instead, I give her the truth. "I've already met you. I don't think the rest of these girls will compare."

Her eyes slide from mine and she goes back to searching her desk, though I can't miss the hint of color rising in her cheeks. "That's inappropriate. I'm your teacher."

"How old are you?"

"Old enough to know better."

The corner of my mouth turns up into a grin. I lean my hands on her desk and level a gaze her way. "But young enough to do it anyway?"

I expect amusement in her eyes when she looks at

me. Instead, I see only fury. "Why is it so hard for your kind to take no for an answer?"

All the humming excitement of being near her winks out. "My kind?"

"Football players."

I straighten up. I'm a big guy. It takes a lot to phase me. But the revulsion in Lilah's eyes sends me reeling. And it makes me back up a step. After everything that happened last year, I should know better. Better than my former "teammates," anyway.

The reality of just how far-reaching and terrible the scandal was—still is—hits me like a defensive lineman on game day. No, not a scandal. That makes it sound smaller than it was. It wasn't a scandal, it was a horrific crime.

Last year during Christmas break, four of my fellow Mustangs raped a girl. It's still hard for me to believe that—those guys were my friends, my mentors—but I know it's true because one of the fuckers filmed it with his phone. A few days later, his jealous girlfriend found it when she was snooping and posted it online.

It didn't take long to go viral. These criminal motherfuckers carried a passed-out girl into the Mustangs locker room, took off her clothes, and then did what they wanted to her. The very idea of it still makes me sick. I never would have believed that someone I knew could do something like that. But it happened, and it's been fucking with my life ever since. And God, the poor girl. It filled me with shame to think of what happened to her.

To make matters worse, Coach Moe Foster—formerly beloved, legendary, local hero MoFo—went on national television to defend these guys. The quote the media used to skewer him was, "These young men are under a great deal of stress and pressure, and sometimes they act out in inappropriate ways." Social media had a field day with that one. #MSUstressrape is probably still trending.

For those of us on the team, it continues to be a goddamn nightmare. The four rapists were all seniors, all key members of the team, and they were all suspended right before the BCS National Championship game. We lost, of course, and it wasn't long before MoFo was dismissed amid a firestorm of criticism. So now we're scrambling to put together a squad under this new guy, Coach Prescott. So much for our championship hopes.

A lot of the sportscasters say it'd be a shock if we win a single game. And that's nothing to the fans and locals. On one side, there are asshats saying we should bring back MoFo even though he condoned rape; on the other side are the dickwads saying we should get rid of football entirely. All this talk, all this bullshit, all these outsiders who think they know my team.

I'm tired of it.

Lilah is staring at me, every accusation plain to see in her eyes. "I see," I say, my voice cold with sarcasm. "So because I play football, I'm automatically a rapist."

"I didn't say that."

"But that's what you meant." I take another step back from her desk.

She tosses her head, elegantly rude. "I don't know. All the rapists I know are football players, so I guess I'm suspicious of you all."

I don't know what I would have said to her, but at that moment the door opens and a couple of new students walk in. Lilah promptly leaves me hovering in front of her desk, feeling like a fool.

For approximately the billionth time, I curse Jeremy Hudson and his fucking cronies, the assholes who ruined a young woman's life as well as the reputation of my team. Here is yet another way in which their actions have tainted my life: The Mustangs logo on my T-shirt is enough to make a woman afraid of me.

I stalk toward the back of the class and choose the seat farthest away from Lilah. Goddammit. I've really been looking forward to this class. My high school didn't have much of an art program, and since I came to MSU I've been busy with establishing myself on the team. But now it's my senior year, and if I don't learn now, I never will. This year feels like my last chance … for a lot of things.

When I sit down, I feel something in my pocket jab into my leg. It's my latest project—a tiny figurine I've been whittling out of a chunk of cottonwood. I like to keep my hands busy. I carry a chunk of wood and a small chiseling knife pretty much everywhere.

I work a little, letting the wood settle my mind as the class fills in over the next few minutes. It looks like there are about a dozen of us, mostly artsy-looking freshmen and sophomores. I think I'm the only person in this room who has never worn skinny jeans. I know what my dad and uncles—hard-working country boys—would say about these kids.

Probably the same thing they would say about me, if they knew I was taking this class.

Lilah glances up at the clock, which is just striking the hour. I lay the figurine on the desk and tuck my chisel in my pocket, wanting to give her my full attention. She may have decided I'm scum, but that doesn't mean I need to act like it.

"Welcome, everyone, to Introduction to Art. In this class, we'll be studying techniques of various mediums, as well as the foundations of artistic theory. Now, some of you may have been expecting Professor Carlson, but he asked me to fill in this summer. My name is Lilah Stone. I am a local artist here in Granite." She glances down, as if embarrassed. "Some of you may know me as last year's recipient of the Pitkin Prize."

An impressed murmur rustles around the room. *This Pitkin thing must be a big deal.*

"I'd like to get to know you all a bit before we get started," she continues. Just in case I wasn't already hot for her—despite her assumptions about me—she pulls a pair of black-rimmed reading glasses out of her bag to study her class list.

I curse myself for being a sex-obsessed monster, especially after what she just called all football players, but I've always had a thing for girls in glasses. Some irrepressible, insane part of me can't stop imagining Lilah beneath me, those glasses askew as she moans.

Lock that down, Lotto, I scold myself. This woman has made her lack of interest clear.

"Why don't we go around, and you all can tell us a little about what brings you to this class," she says. She glances at me, then away, and turns to a girl sitting on the other side of the room. "Would you start?"

I try to get a hold of myself as each of the students introduces themselves. I've been attracted to girls before, and plenty of them have been attracted to me. I definitely don't need to be lusting after my teacher, one who clearly has some strong thoughts about the Mustangs. I guess I shouldn't be surprised—people have been judging us and doubting us ever since the scandal broke.

Including my new art teacher. But if I don't take this class now, I probably never will.

Fuck.

The door swings open in the middle of some freshman's monologue about how creativity is under-appreciated in higher education.

"Whoa, I'm late?" Reggie Davis, a teammate, comes blustering into class. His words are muffled around the last bite of a breakfast burrito, and he tosses the foil wrapper toward the trash can as the door slams shut behind him. The entire class just stares. "You guys didn't wait for me?"

Great. What is Reggie doing here? If there was ever a stereotypical dumb jock, Reggie is it. He is also one of my fellow Mustangs—a fun-loving, larger-than-life cornerback.

Naturally, he notices me right away. "'Sup, Lotto," he says with a grin. He drops his bag onto the table where I sit and doesn't even attempt to lower his voice as he says, "Sweet, man, you're in this class? I figured, you know, art. How hard can it be?"

CHAPTER THREE
Lilah

Two? Two fucking football players in my very first class? The universe has a shitty sense of humor.

I have zero chill when it comes to football players. The scandal that broke last year was just the icing on a lifetime of irritation at the way football is treated in this town. I've been out at a bar when a group of football players show up, and you'd think the president was in town from the way people act. I couldn't care less about the games, but I keep track of the team schedule because it's impossible to get anything done in town while the Mustangs are playing. I just can't believe how much time and attention people waste on a stupid game.

And that was before four players raped a girl who had gotten too drunk at a party. The video, which has been watched millions of times, spurred a media firestorm about rape culture in sports. That would all be enough to ruffle my feminist feathers, but my fury actually comes from a deeper place.

In the video—which I wish, passionately, I had never seen—a girl is clearly visible, her naked body laying sprawled on a bench, her head dangling at an awkward angle. She's clearly insensate, and her body is marked with red spots where they've pinched and bit and spanked her. She is utterly exposed, utterly powerless, utterly alone.

The girl is Natalie, my best friend since childhood.

They were punished, at least. All four of them are in jail, and Coach MoFo is gone. The team was stripped of their past Pac-12 Championship wins, and they suffered a humiliating loss on national television at the BCS National Championship game. Half of the incoming freshman withdrew their letters of intent. The team has been gutted, and some have said the program is unsalvageable.

Good. None of that is enough. Because after months of being subjected to media scrutiny, being called a slut and a victim, months of knowing that the entire nation had seen her naked and vulnerable, Natalie killed herself.

And I'm nowhere near over it.

"Sit down," I snap, before I get a hold of myself. I have already made a mistake by sniping at the first football player—Riley, he'd said—and I don't want to repeat it. The things I said to Riley were way out of line. He could easily report me to the head of the department for my behavior. I didn't necessarily want this job, but I also don't want to get fired after my first day.

"You got it, sweetheart," the second football player says. "Tell me something … are we going to be painting any nudes?"

A titter of uncomfortable laughter whisks around the room.

Beside Reggie, Riley shifts in his seat. "Reggie, you

asshole, sit the fuck down," he rumbles.

Reggie shrugs and drags a chair over to Riley's table the collapses into it. Riley shoots me a look of chagrin, but doesn't hesitate to make room for Reggie. Typical. Football players stick together, even when one of them is clearly a jerk.

That makes Riley a jerk too. Even if he is the hottest jerk I've ever seen.

I take a calming breath and turn to the rest of the class. "Now that we know each other, let's get started," I say, pointedly ignoring Riley and Reggie even though I didn't give them a chance to share why they're in the class. I'm pretty sure Reggie answered for both of them. I force a smile and say, "The first thing we are going to talk about is the different types of paint."

Soon, I lose myself in the joy of discussing the different uses of oil paints, watercolors, and acrylics. It gives me a small thrill to see that several students are taking notes. I honestly can't wait to tell Gamma about that. Despite my misgivings, I'm finding my first teaching experience surprisingly comfortable. As long as I keep my eyes off the hulking football players sitting in the back of the room.

I can't ignore them completely, though. Oddly, Riley is one of the people taking notes, and I can feel the focus of his attention like a spotlight. Something about him gives me the impression that he approaches everything with the same intensity he's now directing toward me. It makes unwelcome licks of awareness tickle my skin.

Some of that is discomfort having two reminders of Natalie's rape right here in the room with me.

Some of that is shame. As much as I hate to admit it,

I've pre-judged him by the actions of his fellows, and that's not right.

And most disconcerting of all, some of that is arousal. Because having this big, sexy man focused completely on me is making my libido go haywire.

"So now we've talked about the different types of paint and their purposes, but there's really no way to understand how each one works until we try it. I want you to get a taste of each before we focus on them individually. Let's start with the acrylics. I've got some primary colors set up in the back of the room, along with some paper plates and brushes. Go ahead and get a few squirts of each color and meet back at your easels."

It is so weird to watch the entire class obey me. I can see why Marty likes teaching. It's good for the ego.

My inflated sense of power is suddenly punctured when a scuffle breaks out at the back of the room.

"What the fuck, man?" Reggie says loudly. "I was just fucking around."

Riley is standing in front of him, clearly furious. "Just keep your mouth shut, okay?"

"What? What did I say?"

Riley glances at me and lowers his voice, but I can still hear him say, "You know you can't say shit like that, bro. Haven't you learned anything from the gender sensitivity classes?"

"Dude, it would be insensitive not to state the fact that—"

Riley shoves Reggie before he has the chance to state his fact. Before I can even move, Reggie stumbles back, knocking over a huge bottle of red paint. But he doesn't back down—in seconds, he's facing off with Riley like two warring gorillas.

The rest of the students cower back from them, and I don't blame them. Reggie is muscular and large, but Riley makes him look like a lightweight. His aggressive stance makes me suddenly very aware of the size of his hands, the strength of his arms. Some weak, female part of me pulses at the blatant display of masculine power.

But the rest of me isn't having any of this shit.

"Get out. Both of you."

Riley turns to me, his aggression replaced by shock. "What?"

"I don't tolerate fighting in my class. Both of you, get out."

CHAPTER FOUR
Riley

Lilah all but slammed the door behind me as I stumble behind Reggie into the hall.

"You fucking asshole," I start. "I can't believe you just got me kicked out of class."

"Whatever, dude," Reggie says. "I can't believe you're being such a dick about a couple of jokes."

"A couple of—dude, what makes you think I want to hear your running commentary on which of the chicks in that class you would fuck?"

Reggie scoffs. "What? Don't tell me you weren't thinking about the same thing," he says with a shrug. "What else am I supposed to do? Listen to some boring-ass lecture about paint? I don't need that shit."

I grip my head in my hands and pace the hallway. Dammit. I've been looking forward to this class for months, and somehow I manage to fuck everything up on the first day. "I seriously can't believe you can be such an idiot. You're on academic probation, Reg."

"So what else is new?"

"Don't you care about getting an education?"

Reggie smirks. "I'm here to play football. Class is

just to pass the time between practices."

"Dude. That's ridiculous." I've known Reggie for years, and I know there's no real malice in him. But he can be so dense. "So fine, whatever, you don't care about your education. But you still can't say shit like you were saying. Didn't you learn anything from all these consent and sensitivity classes we've been taking?"

"I could be the most sensitive guy on earth and still notice the titties on that professor. Hot damn."

I shake my head, embarrassed at how much his reaction echoes my own. "What if somebody heard you? Did you think of that? After all this shit in the media, don't you think it might make the team look bad if someone knew you were talking that way?"

For the first time, Reggie looks worried. "Nobody heard, Lotto. I wasn't talking that loud."

Reggie only had one speaking volume. And it sure as shit wasn't quiet. I force myself to take a breath and stare at my teammate.

"I heard. And I say that's bullshit. I don't want to hear you talking that way about Lilah."

Reggie raises his eyebrows. "Sorry, dude. My bad. I didn't know you had a thing for her."

"I don't—that's not—it's not about that. She's a human being, you know? She deserves to be treated as more than a sex object."

"All right, Riley, calm down." Reggie's use of my real name is my first clue that he's taking me seriously. "I won't talk about her again."

He's taking me seriously, but still not really getting it. "It's not about her. You shouldn't be saying that shit about any girl."

Reggie's usual goofy attitude returns. "If I ever stop

pointing out gorgeous titties, you'll know something is wrong with me."

I can only shake my head again. Sometimes Reggie is impossible. "What are we going to do about this?"

"About what?" He frowns like he honestly doesn't know what's wrong.

"We got kicked out of class."

"Eh, whatever. I usually ditch most of the semester anyway. Hey, man, college is for fun and girls and football," Reggie argues when I shoot him an incredulous look. "You ought to relax more, Lotto. Get your dick wet."

"Jesus Christ, Reggie. We just talked about this. You can't say shit like that."

"Like what? 'Get your dick wet?'" Reggie claps me on the shoulder with a mock serious look on his face. "She really should be wet and ready, Lotto. Didn't you learn anything from the sensitivity training?"

I shove off his hand and then motion down the empty hallway. "I'm going to wait here. I want to apologize to the teacher."

Reggie raises one eyebrow and snorts. "Sure, dude, whatever. I'll see you at practice later."

Since it's summer, the new coaching staff has to keep full-contact practice limited, and training camp isn't for another month, but that doesn't stop us from getting together a couple evenings a week to run some informal drills. "All right, see you then."

He saunters off down the hall and leaves me alone with my thoughts. It's a two hour class, which means I have almost ninety minutes to wait. Well, that's what the Internet is for. I sit with my back against the wall, pull out my phone, and start to google.

An hour and a half later, the door opens and the class files out. From their excited chatter, I guess I missed a good class. A couple of them cut me dirty looks, but I pointedly ignore them. I don't care about convincing *them* to like me.

Lilah is surveying a row of drying canvases propped against the wall. The canvases aren't much, just early experiments in mixing color, but Lilah is looking at them with stark emotion on her face.

Up until this moment, I realize, I've been caught up by her bright clothes and bold hair. But now I'm catching a glimpse of the woman within, and she's even more fascinating than the one I've already met.

She whirls around suddenly as if she senses me. Our eyes meet, and I can see hers are damp. But then she blinks, and the tender woman is encased in armor.

"Are you here to drop this class?"

"No." I square off, digging my feet into the wood floor. "I want to apologize for my behavior today."

"Do you think an apology is enough for fighting in my class? You spilled half a gallon of red paint."

"I'll clean it up."

"It's already done," she says tartly. "I was planning on teaching cleaning techniques at the end of class, but you and your friend changed that."

Ah. That explains some of the dirty looks I got. "I would have cleaned it up."

"I wasn't going to let paint sit on the floor for an hour."

Shit. "How can I make it up to you?"

Her eyes flicker over me and I wonder, for one glorious second, if she's thinking of making me work for her affection in the most personal of ways. Then she meets my eyes. "I'm not sure you can."

"Give me a chance. I really want to take this class."

"Why?"

I rough my hands through my hair, trying to find the words I've never said to anyone. "I grew up on a farm, and I've been playing football my entire life. There's not much room in my life for ... beauty. I might not have another chance to study art. I might not be any good at it, but I'd like to try."

Her face is still closed. "What about your friend?"

I can't hide my wince. "Not so much. But he's on his own."

"I thought football players stick together."

I point at her and walk closer. "There it is. That's your problem. You are determined to hate me because I'm a football player."

"You've given me plenty of reason to dislike you all on your own."

"What? Spilling the paint?" I shrug. "That was Reggie. I just gave him a little nudge to get him to shut up about ... to make him pay attention."

"It's not just that."

I take another long step closer to her. She answers by taking three quick steps back until her butt hits her desk.

Her movement makes shock flare in my stomach. "Are you afraid of me?"

Her mouth trembles open, then closes again. "I'm not sure."

"Because of what happened last December? I had nothing to do with that."

"So you say."

I have to look away. My desire for her is at war with my frustration. "This is bullshit. I am nothing like those guys. I would never, ever hurt a woman."

She shakes her head, crossing her arms across her delectable chest. "It's not just you. It's the whole culture of football. Nothing matters except winning, and if you are winning nothing else matters. You guys think you can get away with anything. Like your friend. Waltzing into class late, talking during my lecture. It's so arrogant and entitled."

"I see. So I guess you're the kind of person who judges whole groups by the actions of a few."

"That's not ...." She trails off, unable to argue the point.

"Besides, that's Reggie, that's not me." The shock has given way to anger burning inside me, fed by all that hot attraction I feel for her. "You're an artist, right? Well, all the artists I've heard of are drug addicts or insane. Which are you?"

She fixes me with a furious look. "Neither."

"So what does that leave? One-trick pony? Has-been?" She flinches, and I can't help but cruelly home in on it. "You're awfully young to have peaked already."

I probably shouldn't take so much pleasure in her gasp of shock, but hey, I'm not perfect. As evidenced by the fact that my cock actually stirs when her eyes glitter as she stalks toward me.

"You would know at all about peaking, wouldn't you? Playing college football ... this is probably the best your life will ever be."

That shaft hits home. I'm good at football. There's no one out there that'll disagree with me on that. But one bad injury, and my career will be over before it ever really starts. Then what? Is it back to the family farm and a life of looking backward? But I'm not about to admit that to Lilah.

"You're making some major assumptions about a guy you just met."

"I've seen enough," she hurls back at me. "You come in here, expecting me to fall all over myself because you're a football player. Like I'm supposed to be impressed that you're good at throwing a ball."

I cock my head. "Actually, my specialty is knocking people down."

Her gaze drops to my broad chest and shoulders, down my muscular arms. I know I'm built—I work my ass off to stay that way. I can't help but flex a little for her, and I'm rewarded with a flush in her cheeks before her eyes skitter back up to meet mine. "Yes. Um … yes, I imagine you are quite good at that. But that sort of skill isn't going to be necessary in this class."

"How do you know what kind of skills I have?" Her reaction has turned my anger to arousal. I know she's hot for me. I can see it in her eyes, her face. "Maybe I can give you a demonstration."

All it takes is one long stride, and my body is brushing hers.

This time she doesn't back down. My gaze flicks down to her slick red lips. A woman has never instantly hated me before. It stirs my competitive instincts. Her lips are parted, her skin flushed, her spicy scent swirling around me. Some wild, hungry part of me wants to take that plush mouth with mine, whether she wants it or not.

That thought has me stepping abruptly back from the desk. "I'm sorry if I … I'm sorry. If you felt threatened or disrespected. I never intended to make you uncomfortable. I'm sorry."

"You're ... sorry?"

Worried that she'll take this as another reason to kick me out of the class, I shift into conciliatory mode. "Look, I really want to take this class. I'm happy to do some extra credit, or make up this class—whatever you want."

She stares at me for a long moment. "No matter what your friend said, this isn't going to be an easy class. I'm not going to give you an A just to keep you eligible."

"Oh, believe me. I don't expect it to be easy. And I'm willing to work for it."

I hadn't meant it as an innuendo, but heat flushes her cheeks again. "And no more of that. I'm your teacher. We can't keep ...." She waves her hands between us—probably trying to waft away the sexual tension. "I don't know what game you're playing, but ... stop playing it."

A deep breath fills my lungs. Along with the rest of the Mustangs, I've been taking consent and sensitivity classes for months. I've always admired and respected women, but these classes have really opened my eyes to the sort of struggles women have on a daily basis. I have never, *could* never, will *never*, force myself on a woman. I'm not about to start now.

"Okay." I allow myself one last look—one searing moment when I allow myself to think about all the ways I want her, all the ways I can take her and be taken—and then I shut it down. "You don't have anything to worry about."

For a moment, she looks bereft, but then her chin hardens. "Fine. Then you can continue in this class. But I want to see an essay from you by Wednesday about the benefits and drawbacks of using acrylic paint, as well as a survey of one masterwork in acrylic."

"No problem," I say, though it's going to be a lot of work. "Thank you."

She gathers her bags. "I will also expect you to keep your friend Reggie in line."

That sounds quite a bit harder than her first assignment, but I nod. "I'm not sure how often he's planning on coming to class."

I catch the roll of her eyes before she slips on sunglasses. "When he's here, then. I won't have him disturbing the class again."

"Understood."

"Okay. Well, then, I suppose you can stay."

A smile breaks over my face. "You won't regret this."

She sighs as she ushers me out of the classroom so she can lock the door behind us. "I hope not."

CHAPTER FIVE
Riley

I BLINK SWEAT OUT OF my eyes, feeling my face twist into a grimace of effort. My biceps are shaking, my pecs quivering. My body is screaming at me to give up, back down, tap out.

"C'mon, Lotto," Weston Sawyer says, his serious face suspended over mine. "You can do this, man."

I look up at West and think, *Can I?*

As if he can hear my thoughts, West starts stamping his feet in a quick one-two beat, like the clop of a horse. Even through the strain, that's enough to make me smile.

Everyone in the weight room knows what that means. We're the Mountain State Mustangs, and that sound has echoed through our stadium for generations. It takes only a few seconds to have nearly every guy in the weight room stamping his feet so loud it sounds like a stampede.

I haven't heard that sound in months. Despite everything that has happened with the scandal and the team, it has never failed to pump me up. Yet still, my arms shake. I've managed to lower the weight bar to my chest, but my biceps won't obey the command to press, press, press.

Weston's fingertips hover under the bar. West's our new quarterback since Jeremy Hudson was suspended and disgraced, and he's just the kind of guy we need leading our team. Honorable, selfless, loyal. So what if he totally blew the BCS National Championship game last year? I like him anyway.

Through the cacophony, I hear him say, "One time, Lotto. One more."

An image flashes in my mind of my father, spotting me the same way West is doing now. "One more, Riley," he would say. "You have to earn it."

I wasn't going to let my father down. Or West. Or my team.

With every ounce of strength I have left, I force my biceps into motion. My muscles tremble with effort, my arms and chest scream. I can't help the sounds coming from my throat. Grunts and growls seem to have taken the place of breathing. Finally—*finally*—I extend my arms all the way, holding 345 pounds of raw weight in the air.

"Fuck, yes!" West shouts, gripping the bar tight and helping me guide it into the hooks.

Triumph shoots through me. I just bench-pressed the equivalent of the old sow on my family farm. Not bad for a country boy.

"I knew you could do it, man," West says as he pulls me up to sitting. "That's a new team record."

I can barely hear him over the cheers and shouts from the guys in the weight room. A smile spreads over my face. For the first time in a long while, with all my teammates around me, it feels like it used to, playing for the Mustangs. Encouraging, satisfying …

even fun. It feels good to celebrate something together, even if it's as small as a successful bench press.

For a few minutes I'm surrounded by smiling faces as the guys on the team congratulate me. There are a lot of new faces, guys who I've never worked out with before. Technically, it's the off-season, but Coach MoFo always said that great football players never stop hitting the gym. He was wrong about a lot of things, but he was right about that. We're all working out harder than ever to make sure we're in great shape for the start of training camp and the first game.

That's the first step to rebuilding our shattered reputation.

"Hell yeah, Lotto. You're gonna be the biggest guy on the field this year," Reggie says, slapping me on the back.

"Big isn't everything," Ben Mayhew calls out, his breath short as he pushes through a punishing set of burpees. He's a wide receiver, one of the new players Coach Prescott has had to scrounge up since half the expected recruits chose other colleges after the scandal. He's British and apparently was a star rugby player at his university. He's also apparently from some famously upper-crust family, but all that breeding didn't give him any manners.

Ben stands up and stretches before he eyes me. "Fast is just as important as big."

"Oh, yeah?" says Reggie. He hasn't come to art class since the first day, and we've made a tacit agreement not to mention it to the rest of the guys. They would be on his case about risking his eligibility, and they would be on my case about taking an art class.

Neither one of us wants to make it a big deal.

Reggie watches as Ben drops down into a push-up position. In a flash, Reggie grabs hold of Ben's shorts and the back of his shirt and hoists him into the air. "Is fast helping you now?"

Ben thrashes in the air like a swimmer while the guys laugh.

"Put him down," I say, stepping toward them. Reggie's funny, but he can be a jerk without knowing it. The whole incident in class is a shining example of that.

"Aw, Lotto, I'm just having fun with my new roomie." For the past six months, ever since Jeremy Hudson was kicked off the team and out of school, Reggie had been living roommate-free in a double room where all the players live. I guess Coach Prescott finally assigned him a roommate. I feel bad for the guy, being forced to figure out how to live with someone new. But not that bad.

Idly, I pinwheel my long arms to stretch my aching muscles. "You don't start working out and quit fucking around, you're going to have a real fun time this season."

"What do you mean?" Reggie asks, lifting and lowering Ben as the Brit curses and kicks. "This is a workout."

"Enough," I say, over the laughter of my teammates. Ben hasn't been around long, but he hasn't exactly been making friends. Dammit if he isn't as fast as he boasts on the field, though.

"I don't need your help, you big bastard," Ben says, as furious as a spitting cat.

I raise an eyebrow. At my size, there aren't a lot of guys who will insult me to my face. Especially when

I'm trying to help them out.

"Put him down," I repeat mildly, not interested in a fight.

Reggie sighs theatrically and lowers Ben to the ground. But his voice is suddenly serious when he eyes Ben. "When someone breaks a team record, show some respect."

Ben scrambles to his feet. His face is red and his eyes flare with anger as he shoves Reggie back a step. "Don't touch me again. I don't need this shite."

Just like that, the celebratory mood shatters. The weight room falls into a wary silence as Reggie steps toward Ben, his hands curling into fists. I push myself between them, West right there with me.

"Guys, simmer down," the quarterback says, his tone forced into calm.

Muscles in Ben's arms quiver. "Then make that dumb oaf fuck off and leave me alone."

"You think acting like this is going to make me *stop* making fun of you? Dude, you're hilarious. I'm gonna love pissing you off." Reggie gives Ben a shit-eating grin that would make pretty much anyone want to take him out. Ben is no exception. He tries to shove West aside so he can get at Reggie.

Oh yeah, these guys are going to get along great.

I step forward, all trace of a smile wiped from my face. "Cut that shit out, both of you. You could be kicked off the team for fighting with each other. That's the last thing we need right now."

"Lotto's right," West says, laying a hand on both of their shoulders. "We have to work together. This sort of petty infighting isn't going to win us a championship."

Ben shakes West's hand off. "There's no way this

team can win a championship," he scoffs, then stalks out of the gym.

In his wake, all the buoyancy drains out of the room. It's obvious: Everyone wonders if Ben is right. It used to be that if you were a Mustang, you could count on at least being competitive for a Bowl game, being ranked in the top three in the conference. But this year ... some of our best players have left for other schools, we have a brand new coach who is a stranger to all of us, and our quarterback has only played one Pac-12 game and it was a brutal loss. Our upcoming season will be the toughest we've ever played, and we're hardly ready to play it.

"Well, that went well," I say to West, who just sighs.

"Let's get back to work," he says shortly, "and prove that asshole wrong."

I work through my ab routine and my cool-down while the team continues working out around me. Gradually, the relaxed atmosphere returns, but I can tell from the way that some of the guys are looking at West that they're still thinking about what Ben said.

Can we win a championship? Hell ... can we even win a single game?

The scalding hot shower beats down against my sore shoulders. I believe in Weston, and I have high hopes in the new coach, but ... I can't shower away the worry that I've made a huge mistake by staying with the Mustangs.

Last year, after the scandal broke, I was approached by a couple of other colleges looking to add more muscle to their offense. NFL scouts like players from winning teams, and if I'm not on a winning team this year .... For the first time, I'm afraid there's a real possibility I won't get drafted. Has loyalty screwed my chances at playing pro?

But the Mustangs are my family ... literally. My father and uncles were all on the team twenty years ago, when the Mustangs were becoming the team to watch. I talked it over with my dad last year when recruiters started sniffing around, and we agreed that I should stay with the Mustangs. Well, I decided, and I convinced my dad it was the right choice. I was so certain that we could come together and make something magical out of this terrible year.

I don't feel that way anymore.

The rape scandal shocked me to my core. I would never have believed it if it hadn't been caught on tape. And what does that say about me, that I would have stood up for these guys who did such a terrible thing? Who might have done that sort of thing more than once? Lilah wasn't wrong when she talked about the mentality that winning excusing all kinds of bad behavior. It makes me ashamed to be part of it.

I turn in the tight shower stall, brushing against the curtain. I let the water pound my chest, idly soaping my armpit. Even though she's been distantly polite during classes the last three weeks, my confrontation with Lilah on the first day of class still haunts me. It pisses me off that she pre-judged me, but the more I think about it, the less I blame her.

She has a point about football players. Some of us are arrogant bastards who take their fame and talent for granted. And more than that, the free education. Thousands of people would kill to attend MSU. Yet look at Reggie. I love the guy, but he's throwing away four years of an education that would cost someone else nearly a hundred thousand dollars for that same slip of paper. But because he's built like a wall and has cinderblocks for shoulders, the administration always seems to find a way to keep him on the team. And it's not just him. I know lots of guys who get away with shit that would get a normal student kicked out of school.

And I'd have to be a moron not to acknowledge that physical and sexual assault is part of that. People tend to believe that when a woman accuses a sports player of rape, she's doing it for attention or money. Nobody wants to believe that a guy you cheer for, you idolize, is capable of hurting a woman. But from O.J. to Ray Rice, there's plenty of evidence that some of those accusations are true.

It never really bothered me before last year's scandal. I knew I would never do something like that, so I didn't really care about it. But now … now that I've joked and laughed and played with guys who turned out to be monsters, it's totally changed football for me. Now, if I can stay healthy and get drafted, do I even want to play pro?

But if I don't try for the NFL, what else am I supposed to do? I'll be graduating this spring with a degree in Ag Science, and pretty much the only place I can take that is back to the farm. As much as I love my family and my hometown, I don't know if I can go back. I spent high school the local hero for my ability on the field. I'm a goddamned god to some in the town now that I play for MSU. And if I go back …. I shake water out of my hair and scrub hands down my face. I don't even want to think about being a failure in their eyes. And not just the townies. My dad and uncles have dreamed of my professional sports career since I was born. Disappointing them would be terrible.

Even though I'm working harder than ever this season, I can't shake the nagging feeling that I'm living a life I don't want. Everything seems tainted by the scandal last year. I can't stop thinking about the way Lilah stumbled back from me the first time I approached her. It kills me, remembering that for just a second, she seemed afraid of me.

Especially since she has been anything but afraid ever since. Every class, she gets more incredible. Not everyone in the class is a beginner like me, but no one even comes close to her innate talent. And she has a way with the students—I'm not the only one mesmerized by her casually brilliant aura. I know this is her first semester teaching, but she's a natural.

She's a natural, and I'm ... I'm not sure what I am. When I walked in for the second day of class, the carving I'd been working on that first terrible day was suddenly sitting on her desk. I must have dropped it during the paint debacle. Claiming it crossed my mind, but it seemed silly to get proprietary about a piece of wood. I carve dozens of these things a year, and my dorm room is filled with them. But I could do better than that unfinished owl.

So the next class, I brought in a carving I'm proud of. It's a delicate willow tree that looks just like the one outside my window at home. Scalloping the leaves had taken forever, but I liked the effect it made in the end. When Lilah wasn't looking, I left it on the top shelf of a supply cabinet where she couldn't help but find it. The next class, it was sitting on her desk next to the owl.

Seeing my work—my *art*—displayed by someone amazing like Lilah filled me with pride. Over the last two weeks, a deer, her fawn, a wizard in robes, and a chubby piglet have joined the tree and owl. I have been having way more fun than I should admit hiding them around the classroom, palming them as I retrieve supplies for our various projects. She never asks about the figurines, and I never volunteer that I made them. I just want her to have a piece of me that I don't really share with anyone else.

I soap my way down my chest, thinking about Lilah. True to my word, I had made no attempt to flirt with her. She treats me like the rest of the students. I shouldn't be thinking about a relationship anyway—this upcoming season will be the most important one of my life, and I really need to concentrate.

But none of that makes a difference. I'm still insanely hot for her.

She seems to have an endless wardrobe of sexy skirts that show off her legs and silky tops that make me wild thinking about the skin underneath. I could spend hours stroking the tattoo that spirals up her arm, kissing the rings and studs lining her ears, tangling my hands in her wild hair. I can't stop thinking about how the sandalwood of my skin tone would look against the ebony of hers.

My cock's rising now, just thinking about her, and my soapy hand slides ever lower. I prick up my ears, straining to hear any movement in the locker room. Empty. I don't make a habit of jacking off in a semi-public place, but there is no way I can go to class in this state. I close my eyes, take my cock in my hand, and begin to stroke.

Immediately, my mind floods with images of her. Her leg hitched up against the desk, laughing, as sunlight pours through the windows. Wearing her glasses, blending watercolors. The lacy pink bra strap that peeks out from her dress during the class. Then my imagination takes over, and I lose myself dreaming of her soft lips, her heavy breasts, her wet, hot pussy.

I've never lusted after a girl like this. But I can't seem to hold back. Every time her eyes find mine during a lecture, my system floods with heat. Every time she stands near me to look at my work, my cock swells against my tight boxer briefs. Once, she laid her hand on my back as she was demonstrating a technique, and I wanted to flip her over and fuck her blind right there on the table.

Fantasizing about that—her legs wrapped around me, my face buried in her breasts, the rest of the students cheering us on—I stifle a groan as I come.

I rest my head against the wall of the shower, breathing like I'd just run the forty. Now that my head is cleared of lust, a peculiar mix of shame and amusement washes through me. I feel like a randy teenager. And if I don't get a move on, I'm going to be late for class.

CHAPTER SIX
Lilah

Riley fucking Brulotte is driving me crazy.

I'm pretty sure it doesn't show on the outside. I'm pretty sure I'm managing to give this lecture about the techniques of Pop Art painters without betraying the heat that pulses through me every time I look at him. Which I hardly ever do, because I can't handle this level of attraction without losing my mind.

I've been teaching this class for three weeks now, and I'm proud to say that it's working out much better than I expected. The projects have been going well, and the students are responsive and engaged. Once I got over my nervousness, it has actually been really fun to go back to basics. I learned most of these techniques a decade ago, and I've been taking them for granted.

Seeing the students get excited about what they are creating has been great. I just wish I could say it's spurred my own artwork. But I've barely sat in front of my easel since class started. I'm too busy researching lectures and putting together lessons. Maybe that's a cop-out, but at the moment it feels like a relief to not be chasing my own creativity.

And I've got enough on my mind trying to ignore Riley. He's sitting at the back of the class, taking notes again. He seems almost too big for the chair, with the way his long arms and legs spread out in every direction. It should look silly, a man his size sitting in a standard classroom chair, but instead he looks calm and confident, like he's hardly aware that he's the biggest man in the room.

He usually wears sweatpants and T-shirts that look thin and soft with wear. These T-shirts have become a source of fascination for me—or, more accurately, the way they cling to his body as he moves. He's got this thick golden hair and sweet brown eyes and a motherfucking dimple, all of which is totally unfair. He should not be allowed to be this hot.

I was hoping that he would be rude or dumb, to counteract the hotness, but so far it doesn't seem like it. In fact, so far he's been attentive and enthusiastic. He asks good questions. The essay he turned in for extra credit was thorough and well-written. And he specifically scheduled a make-up class with me today, after the regular class, to go over the lesson he missed.

All of which makes me feel even worse about the way I pre-judged him. And still—still!—I can't look at him without thinking about the Mustangs who raped my best friend.

It's illogical, but logic has never been a particularly important factor in my life. I run on instinct, emotion. But when it comes to Riley, all my senses are at war.

"All right, so now that we've talked about mixed media, I want you to give it a try on your own. Your homework over the next week is to gather some pictures, items, flotsam and jetsam, whatever, and bring them to class next week. Try to think about composition, and take a look at the selected works by James Rosenquist and Richard Hamilton. We'll start putting together a mixed media piece on Monday."

Every time I say something like that, I get a little thrill. Who would have thought I would ever be the one in charge of a classroom?

I never did particularly well in school—I was always too busy doodling in the margins to listen to my teachers. As an artist, I'm mostly self-taught. Gamma could barely afford supplies when I was growing up, let alone private lessons. Instead, I watched art shows on PBS and read every book I could find. By the time I started winning contests and bringing in a little money, the habit of figuring things out on my own was ingrained.

But now, I'm starting to see what I missed. Being surrounded by other creative-minded people is more fun than I expected. For example, someone has been leaving little hand-carved figurines all over the classroom. They're beautiful and whimsical, and every time I find one it feels like a gift from the universe, just for me. Whoever is making them is incredibly talented. I'm planning on showing them to Marty when he gets back into town. He might be interested in carrying something like this in his gallery. And I get a kick out of the idea of shepherding a young artist.

"Lilah? Do you still have time to do that private lesson?"

I blink myself out of my reverie. I'm glad I asked the students to call me by my first name, but there is part of me that wishes I could change the rules for Riley.

My name sounds too intimate, too warm, on his lips. The slight country twang in his voice always has a powerful effect on me.

"Yes, of course," I say, determined to be professional. "Why don't you grab the acrylics out of the supply cabinet, and I'll grab you a fresh canvas."

During the first class, when I had gone through the basics of acrylics with the rest of the students, I had walked among them so I could see what they were doing. But there is no need to do that today. I perch on a table near his easel so I can watch over his shoulder.

"Okay, so this is a basic lesson in blending and scumbling. Acrylics blend really well when they're wet, and layer really well when they're dry. We're going to experiment a little with both techniques."

"Sounds good," Riley says. "Where should I start?"

"*Hmm*?" I snap my attention back to him and his innocent question. I had been too distracted by the play of muscles in his back. I can think of plenty of places he can *start*. I have to clear my throat before I say, "Just pick a color and paint a patch on the canvas."

"Okay," he says, choosing blue.

This close, his scent wafts around me. He's always shower-fresh, like plain soap and sunshine. I'm pretty sure he goes to the gym before class, which means he must get all hot and sweaty each morning. I can almost imagine him, his hair and shirt dark with sweat, his skin glistening with it, his muscles—

"What now?"

"Uh ...." What was I doing again? "Let's start with blending. Don't clean your brush—just dip it straight into the white. Do you see how the blue comes through when you paint with it? So now, blend that color into what you already have. Do you see how it's easier to blend while the paint is still wet?"

"Yeah."

"So scumbling is a little different than blending. It's a sort of scrubbing motion with your brush, using the side."

"Like this?"

"Not quite." I hop off the desk and walk up beside him. "It's more like this," I say, adjusting his hold on the brush.

"Like this?" he says again, turning his face toward me.

I'm standing closer than I should be, just over his shoulder. We're separated only by the muscle of his arm. This close, I can see that he has a dip in his upper lip that looks perfect for kissing.

"That's fine," I choke out, stepping back. "Do ... do that for a minute."

Jesus, what the hell is wrong with me? It's been a while since I got laid, but I've never felt this hungry and reckless about sex before. And Riley is out of the question as a partner. I don't have to be in love with every man I sleep with, but I probably shouldn't hate some intrinsic part of his life. Football is a big part of him, and I'm not sure I can tolerate that.

Not to mention that I'm his teacher. Yeah, it's just for the semester, but I'm taking it seriously. It wouldn't be right to indulge this momentary lust, not when I have to see him every other day for the next three weeks.

When I dare to look at him again, Riley is still dabbing at the canvas, his brows lowered as he studies the various shades he's creating. "What do you think of working with acrylics?"

"Takes a firmer hand than watercolors," he says, still focused on his work. "But the colors are bolder. Gutsier."

I raise my eyebrows at that description. "Gutsier?"

"Well, harder to blend, at least. I think I've made a mess of it."

I come around to look at the canvas. "No, you're doing great. Do you see the difference between the two techniques? Blending makes the brush strokes more obvious, while the scrumbling has more of a spongy texture. It's great for trees and waves."

"Do you mostly use acrylics?"

"Or oils. You'll like oil paint; it's definitely gutsy."

He smiles, his dimple winking at me. "*First Sky*—the painting that won you the Pitkin—that was acrylics, right?"

"Right. Have you been googling me?"

He shrugs and goes to get more paint. "I had a while, sitting out in the hallway on the first day of class. It's an amazing painting," he says, returning to *First Sky*. He sits back down with the new paint—more shades of blue. "The MOMA website says it's ten feet high and eighteen feet wide. That's crazy big."

I smile wanly. "Crazy big paintings are my specialty."

"I'm pretty sure my phone screen didn't do it justice. How does it feel knowing that thousands of people are looking at your painting every day?"

"Surreal," I say, before thinking. "I never thought I had the chance to win it."

"I looked at your website. It looks like all your stuff is pretty amazing."

Warmth is crawling up my cheeks, and I have to

look away. I have been praised before, I remind myself. "Thanks."

He continues to work for a few minutes. Something about his silent presence invites confession. After a moment, I say, "You weren't wrong, you know. The other day, when you called me a one-trick pony."

"That was a shitty thing to say. I was riled up, and—"

"I said some shitty things to you, too. Don't worry about it. But the truth is … I've hardly painted anything since I won the Pitkin."

He touches me—just the tips of his fingers, tilting up my chin. "Did you lose your mojo?"

I can't help but smile at the term, but it falls quickly. "Sometimes I wonder if my well of talent is dry."

He shakes his head, exhaling out his nose. "Yeah, right. I've never seen anyone as talented as you. When you demonstrate this stuff, you make it look effortless."

"That's just technique."

His hand drifts to my shoulder, its warmth seeping through my blouse. He's still seated at the easel, but even at my perch on the desk he's eye-level with me. It feels close, intimate.

"You'll be that good too, with enough practice," I say, trying to ignore the way my entire body is becoming slowly consumed with heat.

Something makes his brows twitch before he focuses on me again. "I'm not sure how much time I'll have. But I'll always appreciate everything I've learned from you in this class."

"Really?"

"Really."

I'm not sure how it happens. One second, he is

looking at me with his serious, soft eyes. Then his mouth is on mine.

CHAPTER SEVEN
Lilah

Our lips are just brushing, our bodies still inches apart. It's a kiss to float on, to drown in. I part my lips, seeking more, and for an instant Riley dares to meet me.

Then he's pulling away.

"I'm sorry, I'm sorry, shit," he says in a tumble of rough words. "I didn't mean to do that; I know you don't want that from me. I'll just go, I'll just go now. I can still drop the class. Don't worry, you won't have to see me again. I should never have done that without getting your consent, and I—"

"Riley. It's okay." My heart is thundering in my chest. "You don't have to apologize. You didn't force me into anything."

"I didn't?"

My voice hitches a little as I admit the truth. "I wanted that too. I haven't been able to stop—"

His eyes darken with desire, and before I can say the rest, he's swept me up again.

Holy God, that mouth! Fast and strong and soft … devastating. This time his kiss is anything but sweet.

His tongue is clever and insistent, tangling with mine until I'm giving as good as I get. When he finally tears his mouth from mine, I can only moan in protest.

His lips slide down my throat, and his arm wrap me up so closely I have no choice but to arch against him. I can feel my hard nipples rubbing against my slick satin bra, and it's not enough, not nearly enough. I want his hands, his fingers, his mouth.

He has other ideas, apparently. His hands travel down to my ass. He groans when he cups both cheeks in his huge, spread hands. My knees go watery as he nips at my neck. I can feel his erection pressing against my belly—hard and hot and huge.

God, I want to fuck this man. I want him to fuck me right here on this desk until I'm screaming his name.

It's my own shocking desire that makes me shove him away.

"Stop. We have to stop."

The gravelly note in his voice turns me on even more. "Why?"

I stare at him, emotion swirling inside me. His big chest is heaving, the Mustangs logo taunting me.

"I won't," I manage through panting breaths. I can't believe I almost did this, that I almost betrayed my best friend. "I won't have anything to do with a football player."

Without any heed whatsoever for locking up my classroom, I escape out the door.

A bike ride home in the hot afternoon sun does nothing to cool me off. The thoughts in my head chase each other with the same driving rhythm of the pedals.

What have I done?

What am I doing?

What am I going to do?

I want—no, *need*—to dislike Riley. If only he were a lazy, arrogant lunkhead, instead of the hard-working and respectful man he's turned out to be. I'm finding myself opening up to him in a way I haven't since Natalie's death. She was the person I always trusted with my fears and insecurities, since my Gamma never allows me to doubt myself. Natalie listened to my worries, sympathized with my frustration, then always found a way to distract me.

Riley has found a way to distract me, all right. So much so that for a moment back there I completely forgot about the pain his kind caused my best friend.

The media never revealed Natalie's identity, but everyone in Granite knew who she was. And a lot of people didn't want to see their beloved Mustangs destroyed by scandal. Natalie was inundated with hateful messages on social media and dirty looks all over town. She lost her job, lost the guy she'd been dating ... lost herself. And I didn't see it happening.

My eyes are blurry with sweat—maybe tears. I pedal harder.

Football players destroyed Natalie's life. They took everything from her. And I can never, ever forget that.

But I had forgotten it. In my haze of lust, I've ignored all the reasons why I shouldn't be attracted to Riley. I feel weak and pathetic ... like a bad friend.

Because that's the thing: It doesn't matter if she's no longer here. I'm supposed to be Natalie's best friend. That connection wasn't severed by her death. If anything, I've clung to it. I have to keep her memory alive, or a part of me will die.

"Is that you, Lilah?" Gamma calls as I rush through

the door.

"Yeah," I shout, not even bothering to drop my bags. "Going to the bathroom!"

I just can't face my grandmother yet. I need a minute to get my head together.

"You want a snack, honey?" Gamma asks. I can hear her measured step coming down the hall.

"No!" I cast about for a reason to stay in the bathroom. "I'm going to take a shower."

"Okay, hon," she says.

I sit on the edge of the tub and cover my face with my hands. How could I have let this happen? Why *him* of all people? It's just so ... wrong.

I'm holding on to Natalie's memory so tightly that I can't reach for anything else. Riley has reminded me that I'm letting my life pass me by. But how can I move on without abandoning my best friend?

I can't blame Riley for something he didn't do. He wasn't one of the football players who raped her; he wasn't one of the angry fans who drove her to suicide. But blame is all that's holding me together. If I blame football players, I don't have to blame myself for not saving her.

Miserable, I curl in on myself, slinking down to a ball on the floor. I should have been there for her. If I hadn't gone to New York to accept the Pitkin, I would have been home the night she was raped. I could have protected her, and none of this would have ever happened. And then after, even though I tried to be there for her, it still wasn't enough. It wasn't enough to stop her from slitting her wrists.

Now I'm crying in earnest.

She cut deep gouges longways into her flesh. Her parents had tried to get her to go to a movie with them, but she said she wasn't in the mood. When they got back a few hours later, she was long gone. She was alone as she slowly bled to death. The same way she was alone that horrible night when she went to the party.

And now, months later, I can't shake the feeling that I should have known. With all the years of our friendship, I should have been able to sense that she was planning to die. In retrospect, everything seems like a sign. Everything seems like a missed opportunity. Instead, I was sitting on the couch with Gamma watching *Project Runway* at the moment she was ending her life.

I'm not sure I'll ever be able to shift that guilt. Even if I can, I'm not sure I want to.

With a groan, I knock my head against the wall. Why does it have to be Riley? Why can't I have this intense attraction to someone more suitable? I'd be a fool to pretend that his size and strength aren't part of his appeal. But I wish more than anything that he wasn't a football player.

I pull my sketchbook out of my bag. For me, drawing is like therapy. It helps me think through things, think around them. I set my pencil to paper and let it go.

What I draw is his face. Not in the moment before he kissed me, though that image flickers endlessly in my brain. No, I draw how he looks when I give a lecture in class—open, interested, curious. The hardest part of all this is that I genuinely like him, even though I hate everything he stands for. Maybe I'm being melodramatic. He was right when he said I was judging him based on the actions of others. Maybe I'm going about this the wrong way. Instead of pulling away from him, maybe I need to get to know him better.

There's a sharp rap on the door. "Lilah, are you all right? I thought you were taking a shower."

"Yeah, I am," I say, snapping my sketchbook shut. "I was just ... uh ... looking at my phone."

She pops the door open anyway.

"Gamma!"

"Well, I didn't hear the water running, and I was worried. And here you are, sitting on the floor with your makeup a mess."

I swipe under my eyes. "I got sweaty. And my eyes were watering from ... allergies."

"Allergies?"

I shrug. "Or something. I'm going to hop in the shower in a minute."

My grandmother still looks suspicious. "All right. But if you need anything, honey, I'm right here."

She closes the door again. I get up and turn the lock, and hear my grandmother huff before she walks away.

I don't know why I'm being so secretive about Riley. I'm definitely not ready to tell my grandmother that I was ... doing whatever I was doing with a football player. I pick up my sketchbook and peek at the drawing of Riley.

There is something here. Something I need to understand. Despite who he is, despite how I judged him, Riley is the only one who can help this make sense.

CHAPTER EIGHT
Riley

"Hit him, Lotto! Hit him hard!"

I grunt, my cleats tearing up turf as I dig in to drive the tackling sled down the field. My legs and shoulder are screaming, but I keep pushing, pushing, pushing. And the dummy is barely moving.

"Fuck," I say, dropping back.

"What the hell, Lotto," Coach Prescott says, dropping down off the sled. "You got more than that."

"I'm giving it all I've got," I protest, wiping sweat off my forehead.

"Bullshit. Is that what you're going to say when there's a big bastard linebacker snarling at you from across the line?"

"Yes," I say mulishly. I'm hot, tired, and so worked up over Lilah I can't think straight.

"Well, that's not good enough! These boys are depending on you, Lotto. They are counting on you to crush the other team. That is the purpose for your existence on this field, and if you can't do it, then why are you here?"

"Fuck if I know," I spit.

Head in the Game

Football used to be fun, it used to feel like family. But everything feels wrong now, everything feels off.

Coach grabs me by the muzzle of my helmet and pulls my face down to his. "You could be somewhere else. Playing for someone else. Is that what you want?"

I don't know Coach Prescott very well. The school brought in an outsider to replace Coach MoFo, which I suppose makes sense, but none of us quite trust him yet. I don't know how he'll react, but I figure I'll answer with the truth. "I don't know what I want."

He lets go of the helmet's guard. "I know why you're here. Because you *are* good enough. Because you're tougher than any of the rest of the cowards who ran away from the Mustangs when it got hard. You're here because you care."

He makes the last word sound like an insult. "What's wrong with caring?"

"I don't need you to care, I need you to play football!" Coach Prescott paces away, then quickly back. "I don't want your pity or your worries or your concerns or all the tender bullshit that is tearing you up inside. I want your muscle! I want your bones and blood and guts!"

"I'm giving you all I've got!"

"Then prove it!" He jumps back up on the tackling dummy. "Prove it!"

I look up at him, trying to summon even one reason to push myself. Lilah hates football players. Something about that makes me hate myself.

"Fuck this," I say, yanking off my helmet. "I need a break."

"You put that fucking helmet back on, son," Prescott said, his voice dangerously low.

"I don't need this shit," I say, turning to go.

"You walk away now, Riley … you can't come back. It's all over for you."

The use of my real name snags at something in me, and I stop. I can't imagine my life without football. Is that a good thing or a bad thing?

A life with football means a life without Lilah. And as mad as I was at her for being illogical and prejudiced, I'm twice as mad at myself for caring this much about a woman who doesn't want me.

"Put your helmet on, Lotto," Prescott says. "Whatever it is you are feeling, take it out on this sled."

After a moment, I pull my helmet back on. In its familiar cage, I can only see in one direction—toward Coach Prescott. I think about Lilah and the Mustangs and my future and let the pressure simmer inside me. Then, lodging my shoulder against the sled, I let that pressure blow.

"Good!" Coach Prescott shouts as the dummy begins to move. "Great! You're doing great, Lotto!"

I drive forward, telling myself I'm leaving Lilah behind with every step. This is my life. It's always been my life, always *will* be my life, and if she can't deal with me playing football, then fuck her.

By the time I finally collapse, I've driven the sled thirty yards.

"There you go, Lotto. I knew you had it in you."

I tug off my helmet and nod at the coach, too exhausted to speak.

"Now that I know you have that kind of intensity, I expect to see it at every practice."

He claps me on the shoulder before jogging off to another part of the field where Weston is struggling to perfect his spiral.

"What do you think of this guy?" Reggie asks, coming up behind me and tapping me on the shoulder with a bottle of water.

I pour the water down my throat, dumping the last few ounces over my head. The late afternoon Colorado sun is brutal. When I have the energy to speak, I say, "He's got balls, that's for sure."

"He's no MoFo," Reggie says, idly stretching his hamstring.

I don't answer. MoFo was, hands down, one of the best coaches in college football. His eye for talent and creativity on the field was unmatched. There are still plenty of people who want him back at MSU, despite what he did. And I won't deny that there was a certain comfort in knowing that MoFo had the experience and expertise to win football games.

Prescott, on the other hand, is an unknown. He was with a small college for a few years, and turned their football program from a joke into a competitor. I've heard he played college ball himself, until he blew out his knee and had to quit. A lot of people think he's an odd choice to coach on this level, and he's been taking flak for months.

But Coach Prescott just made me dig deeper, pull out more dedication, than I had in a long time. He saw my weakness and convinced me to turn it into strength. Which is exactly what a good coach is supposed to do.

"I like him," I say finally, "but I think it's up to us more than him. Some of these new guys out here, I don't know anything about them. Last year's team was like a well-oiled machine, and this year we're just a bunch of spare parts."

"You're not wrong about that, man. And some of these guys—like Duke Dickwad over there," he says, sparing a glare for the Brit rugby player, Ben Mayhew, "they take themselves way too seriously."

I cast a look at Reggie. I've heard about the recent shit Reggie has pulled in their shared kitchenette. "Is he still mad because you super-glued all his silverware together?"

"Yeah," Reggie says with a huff. "I got him some replacements, but he refuses to use them. He called me a tosser, and I don't need to speak British to figure out what it means. But, I mean, what sort of dude is too good to use plastic forks?"

I raise an eyebrow but decide to move on. "Anyway, we ought to have some sort of bonding exercise where we can all get to know each other better. Like go rafting or camping or some shit." I say it casually, but I want to bond with my new team. Just not in a way that they'll give me shit about.

"Yeah, we could do that," Reggie says slowly, before his face lights up. "Or we could throw a big fucking party tonight."

I start to argue, but when I really think about it, a party sounds like exactly what I need. A few drinks, some good times with guys who accept me. Maybe I can hook up with one of the hotties who always seem to appear at these parties. That would be a good way to clear Lilah out of my system ... and prepare me for the fact that I will see her in class on Monday.

"Yeah," I say. "Yeah, that's a great idea, Reggie."

My cell phone rings just as I'm stepping out of my post-practice shower. I hit the speaker to answer. "Hey, Dad."

Head in the Game

"Riley. I didn't expect to catch you."

"Coach let us out of practice a little early today."

Dad's silence speaks volumes. Finally, he says, "I thought MoFo usually kept you boys until five."

"It was close to a hundred degrees today, Dad. And we've got weights tomorrow morning then practice in the afternoon."

"Well, all right. I just hope this guy Prescott knows what he's doing. It's gonna be hot tomorrow—is he gonna let you off early then too?"

"I don't think so," I say, already knowing how my dad is going to react. "We're actually going to be in the pool tomorrow, doing water training."

"Water training? You mean like aerobics? Like the little old ladies down at the YMCA? Dammit, Riley. I'm gonna get in touch with the school board. This new guy is driving your team into the ground."

"It's actually really hard," I protest, rubbing the towel over my hair before tying it around my hips. "We did it last week. You have to tread water the whole time and control your body in the water. It was a good workout."

"Well, sure, if you're going to be a synchronized swimmer!" My dad's voice echoes around the empty shower stall. "But *you're* going to be a football player, Riley. You should be practicing football."

"I am." I hate how defensive I sound. "My shoulder's sore from pushing a sled all afternoon, okay? I'm getting plenty of football practice."

"I don't know, Riley, I just don't know. What if this guy is the reason you don't make the NFL?"

I pick up my shower caddy and turn off the speaker, bringing the phone up to my ear as I leave the bathroom. "We talked about this. You said you wanted me to stay on the Mustangs."

"I know, I know. But sometimes I wonder if we made the wrong choice."

We? Technically, it was my choice. "Dad, if I don't make the NFL it will be my fault, not Coach Prescott's."

I could almost hear my dad glowering. "We've worked so hard to get here. I've never been prouder than when the Mustangs won the Pac-12 Championship last year. And to have it all taken away from you over something you didn't even do—"

"Yeah, Dad, I know."

"I just want you to have the best possible chance in life, son. I came close to making the NFL, but you—you've got a real chance. You know we're all counting on you, right, son?"

In my room, I collapse onto the narrow bed. The springs squeak under my weight. "Yeah, I know, Dad."

"If you were to get drafted … hell, the town would probably throw a parade in your honor. You know we're all watching you this year. This is your year."

I'm sure my dad means to bolster my spirit, but he's just making me miserable. "Look, Dad, I've got to go. We're throwing a party in the dorm tonight."

My father's tone instantly brightens. "A kegger, huh? That's just what you need. Hell, I remember your uncles and I had a couple of great parties at Taylor Hall back in my day."

"I know, Dad." Everything I've done is like a reboot of my dad's and uncle's time here. I even live in the same football dorm they all did. It's exhausting, sometimes, always being expected to be the bigger, better version of their generation.

"But don't drink too much, all right? If you've got

two practices tomorrow, you need to be ready to show your best. I know you're young, and you think hangovers don't affect you—"

"Okay, Dad. Look, I gotta go, okay?"

"All right, son. Remember—stay focused. We've got a goal, and we're going to achieve it."

"Thanks, Dad. Love you."

"Love you too, son. And love from your mother."

I click the phone off and let it drop to the bed beside me. Talking to my father is exhausting.

Reggie doesn't bother to knock before coming into room. "Dude, Hawaiian theme. Get your ass up and help me decorate."

"I just remembered, I hate parties," I say with my eyes closed.

Through closed eyes, I hear Reggie rifling through some things on my shelf. I crack one eye open just as he's plucking one of the wooden figurines from the back of the shelf. "Is this what I'm missing in art class?"

"It's nothing."

Reggie frowns, staring at the piece. "Did you make this?"

"Yeah, but it's not big deal. I just whittle to keep my hands busy, you know?"

Reggie peers at the figurine. It's one of my more detailed pieces—a football cleat with the laces untied. "Can I have this?"

"Huh? Uh, yeah, I guess." I can always make another.

"Cool. Reminds me of my lucky shoes," he says, pocketing the figurine. "Anyway. Dude. Hawaiian theme. You know what that means? Bikinis. Lots of girls in bikinis."

My mind wonders how Lilah would look in a swim

suit—all those gorgeous curves spilling out of stretchy fabric—and I have to sit up to hide my burgeoning erection. Shit. Even after hours of exercise and a determined effort to banish my attraction to her, she is still the first woman who comes to my mind.

I won't have anything to do with a football player.

Maybe girls in bikinis will be a sufficient distraction. "It's summer, Reg. Where are you going to find girls in bikinis?"

Reggie smirks. "Oh, they'll come. Don't you worry."

I can't argue with that. If anyone knows how to throw a party, it's Reggie. "All right, all right. But keep it tame, okay? Coach wants us in the weight room tomorrow at nine."

"Yeah, yeah. Now get dressed," he says, throwing a plastic object at me.

"What's this?"

"Hawaiian theme, bro," he says as he goes to rouse the rest of the dorm.

CHAPTER NINE
Lilah

I DRESS WITHOUT MY USUAL flair. It's hard to get fresh when you know you're going to eat crow. I need to talk to Riley, and I need to do it now—before I lose my nerve, and definitely before class on Monday.

I owe him an explanation for my behavior. I should never have let our encounter after class verge into personal territory. I'll just explain to him that, for various reasons, I don't think it's a good idea for us to pursue a relationship.

Pedaling back to campus, I practice my little speech. I will be very mature. Very adult. And then we can just go back to being teacher and student, like none of this ever happened.

But when I get to Taylor Hall, I hesitate. It's the dorm in the center of campus where all the football players live. And while the rest of the campus is quiet and empty, Taylor Hall is practically pulsing. The front door is propped open, and music pours out of the open windows. Laughter and conversation seem to be coming from all three floors, and both men and women streaming in and out of the dorm are clutching red plastic cups.

I can guess, from the inflatable palm tree and kiddie pool in the front yard, that they're going for a tropical theme. As I stand there, unable to move, a group of giggling girls in bikinis and sarongs teeter up to the door.

I don't know why I'm surprised to have stumbled into a party here. I've been to my fair share of campus ragers—in fact, I've been to parties in this very dorm, usually with Natalie. But somehow, I thought these sort of parties, with too much booze and too little oversight, would have stopped after the scandal last year. It was just this sort of party where Natalie met the guys who would rape her.

Can I do this? Just waltz into the very place where Natalie started that long, horrible descent? All to reason with some guy? A girl wading in the kiddie pool slips, and her friends just laugh as she falls ass-first into the water.

I want to run up to them and make sure they'll be safe: buddy up, don't drink the punch, never leave a friend behind. I want to remind them about Natalie and all the thousands of girls like her who are sexually assaulted every year. Do they understand how much danger they are in? Horrible things happen when girls don't look out for each other.

Before I do anything, they haul her up and disappear into the dorm. This is such a mistake to be here. I'll should come back tomorrow. Or maybe Sunday. Any time other than a beach-themed party. Between my black skinny jeans and gray tunic studded with metal grommets, I stick out like a black cloud. I *will* talk to Riley, apologize ... but later.

I unlock my bike and am swinging a leg over the

seat when Riley comes running out the door.

"Lilah, wait up," he says, kicking his way through a plastic grass skirt. "I thought that was you. We need to talk."

Time seems to slow down as Riley jogs closer. He's wearing nothing but that grass skirt and a pair of snug boxer briefs. A couple of flowered leis bounce against his chest. That hard, broad, heavily-muscled chest flexes with every movement. Oh, lord. I'm going faint just looking at him.

I've spent all these weeks in class admiring the way his muscles move under his T-shirt. Now I realize my fantasies are nowhere close to reality. As he jogs toward me, his abs flex, his pecs clench, his biceps pulse. Below that, the strips of green plastic cling to his powerful thighs, getting trapped around the heavy bulge in his shorts.

God, this boy is built! Saliva pools in my mouth, and my hands fairly itch with the need to touch all that masculine perfection.

"Hey," he says when he gets close. "I saw you from the window. Are you here for me?"

It takes all of my concentration to nod. I can't stop looking at him. His angled collarbone ... the trail of hair running down from his navel ... his thick forearms, corded with muscle.

"Thank god," he says with a grin. "I forgot how much I hate parties. And since I agreed to this one because I was mad at you, it's your duty to get me out of here."

I'm still poleaxed from the sight of his body. And now he's close enough for me to catch his shower-fresh scent, which makes me want to bury my face in his skin. It takes a minute for the words to penetrate.

"You're mad at me?"

"I was mad at you. Still am, I guess. But I'd rather talk to you than be all resentful and weird."

"You don't want to stay at this party?"

"God, no."

"You live here. All your friends are here. There are a hundred girls in tiny outfits in there."

"Yeah," he says, "it's funny. For some reason, not one of those half-naked girls interests me as much as you do."

I can hear my heart pounding in my ears. "Riley …."

"Look, just keep me company. It's still too early for me to escape to my room and watch Netflix."

I stare at him for a moment. "You really aren't what I expected."

His smile widens. "I'm enjoying destroying your prejudices. Do you know the diner over on Third?"

"Duke's?"

"Yeah, that's the one. I could go for some hash browns." He smiles at me as if there is nothing impossible between us.

For a moment, I want desperately to believe this is true. "Okay," I say. "But you should probably put on some clothes."

He looks down at himself, as if he's forgotten that ninety percent of his glorious body is on display. "I guess I should," he says. "I'll be back in a minute, okay? Don't leave."

I should leave. But the sight of his muscular ass as he jogs back across the lawn strikes me dumb.

"It's fine," I say to myself. "We'll go get something to eat, and I'll explain. It'll be fine. It'll be over."

Which is what I want. Right?

By the time we get to the diner, I feel more solid. He is wearing a shirt, for one thing. Also, he orders milk to drink, which is so silly that it puts me at ease.

Of course, he is still obscenely sexy, sitting across from me in a vinyl booth. But I can handle it. I can control this conversation.

"Riley, I don't want you to get the wrong idea about what happened this morning."

A flicker of surprise runs over his face. "You don't want to make meaningless small talk before you reject me?"

I feel my lips twitch into a smile. "No, I think it's better if we just dive right in."

"Okay," he says, sitting back in the booth. "Dive."

"It was enjoyable, but it shouldn't have happened," I say, my practiced speech coming out in a rush. "I am your teacher, and it's unprofessional. Additionally, I'm not interested in pursuing a relationship with you, so I shouldn't have ...," *kissed you senseless*, I think. "It would be better if we forgot about it and moved on."

He stares at me for a moment. "Yeah ... that's not going to work for me."

"What do you mean?"

"Trying to forget that I kissed you," he says, settling his elbows on the table and leaning in. "I've been thinking about it for hours. Honestly, I've been wanting to do it for weeks, so I'm pretty sure I'm not going to stop wanting you. Do you want me too?"

He is so big, that's the problem—no matter where I look, I'm looking at him. That's why I feel so hot, so buzzy. And now I'm close enough to him to see that his hair is dark underneath the streaks of gold, and that his eyes are a deep, sober brown to counteract that devious dimple.

"Lilah, do you want me too?"

"That's ... beside the point," I say breathlessly.

"No, I think that's precisely the point. I want you. I've had three weeks to fantasize about all the ways I want you, and the list just keeps getting longer and longer." He licks his lips, and it's as if the hot images running through his mind flicker in my head too. "The teacher thing is nothing—it'll be a moot point in a few weeks anyway when the class is over. So that just leaves the fact that you have an irrational hatred of football players."

"It's not irra—"

"Thanks," Riley says, talking over me and smiling at the waitress delivering our food. She has a slice of pie for me, and everything else in the kitchen for him. An enormous plate of eggs and hash browns is accompanied by bacon, sausage, pancakes, a biscuit covered with gravy, and a bowl of fresh fruit.

"Seriously?" I say as a second waitress arrives with a plate of fries.

"I'm a growing boy," he says. "Literally. I'm bulking up right now, trying to get as big as I can for the season."

I've been known to put down a big meal, but I marvel at the number of plates on his side of the table. "There's no way you can eat all that."

He grins. "Watch me. So, where did you go to art school?"

"Huh?"

"Art school. You can't be that much older than I am, so you must be some sort of prodigy, right?"

He's trying to distract me. And it's working. "No—I mean, yes, kind of, but—no. I didn't go to art school."

"Really? You seem to know so much about this

stuff."

"Ahh ...." He's already taken down all of the eggs, three pieces of bacon, and half the pancakes. I pick up my fork and take the first bite of my blueberry pie. "I was planning on going to school, eventually. But then my grandmother had a heart attack. We're managing it, but ... it's a struggle."

"What about your parents?"

"They're not around." There is no way I'm going to tell him about that. Instead, I return to the reason we're here. "I don't have an irrational hatred of football players."

He swallows the last of his pancakes. "What would you call it then?"

"I would call it a learned intolerance for the football lifestyle."

He purses his lips. "Those sure are some fancy words. What do they mean?"

The way he exaggerates his drawl makes me feel both sheepish and defensive. "You know what I mean. Football players think they can get away with anything. Look at your friend Reggie. He expects me to just pass him because he's a football player."

Riley tilts his head. "It's worked for him so far."

"That's my point. He's getting a college degree for nothing. And it doesn't stop there," I say, warming up to my subject. "Football players get away with all kinds of things. I grew up in this town, and I've seen Mustangs get away with drunk driving, vandalism, starting fights in bars. Nobody wants to punish them because everybody wants them playing football on Saturday. It's ridiculous."

"You don't think good kids should get a chance to make mistakes?" He has stopped eating, although there is still food on his plates.

"These aren't all 'good kids.' They get told over and over that there aren't any consequences for their actions. They start to think that they're supposed to get whatever they want. And they don't care who they hurt in the process; they don't care what kind of destruction they leave behind."

He's frowning at me now. "Don't you think that's a broad generalization?"

"Not when football is the excuse for a crime," I say, not able to hide my anger. "Not when four star players think their status should make it okay for them to rape someone."

He points his fork at me. "See, there it is. This is about the scandal last year."

"Of course it is," I say, throwing up my hands. "I can't believe that any woman would trust football players after that. I can't believe that you're still allowed to have drunken parties with vulnerable girls."

"Everybody has to show ID," Riley says quickly. "All the underclassmen have to stay sober, and the girls mix their own drinks."

"And you think that's enough?" My hands are shaking too much for me to eat. "You think that makes up for what happened to Natalie?"

"Natalie?"

I can feel the blood draining from my face. "You don't even know the name of the girl who your teammates raped?"

He shakes his head. "No, no of course I know her name. Everybody knows—"

"Right. Everybody knew she had been raped while she was blackout drunk. Everybody could see her naked on the Internet. Do you have any idea how humiliating that was for her?"

"It sounds like you have some idea." Riley's brown eyes have become so sympathetic it nearly undoes me. "Did you know her?"

I press my lips together. I'm tired of crying, and I'm perilously close to breaking down again. It takes a long moment before I can get the words out. "She was my best friend."

Riley sits back with a sigh. "So that's why. That's why you hate football players."

I could argue the semantics, but I don't think I can go through it again. "Yes. That's why."

He reaches across the table and covers my hand with his. "I'm so sorry about what happened to her."

My face crumples, and I look away.

"But you know I didn't do that," he continues. "I would never do what those guys did. And if I had known at the time, I would have done everything I could to stop it."

"Would you?" I say, peering up at him. "No one else did."

His mouth twists. "Look, maybe you have a point. I'm not stupid, I know that football players have a certain reputation. But it seems really unfair that you assume we're all the same. I'm more than just a football player."

He's right, I'm being unfair. That doesn't mean I can change how I feel. "It doesn't matter. You're my student. We can be friendly, but that's it."

"You didn't answer my question before," he says, waiting until I met his eyes. "If we take away everything else. If it's just you and me ... do you want me?"

The answer, of course, is yes. But I feel like my heart is being torn in half. No matter how much I want him, my guilt over Natalie won't allow it. "I'm telling you I don't want to be in a relationship with you. Please don't push it any further."

He holds my gaze for a long moment, and then he removes his hand from mine. I almost reach for him. "Okay. We can leave it at that."

My tight shoulders relax. Is it relief or regret coursing through me? "Thank you."

"Oh, don't thank me," he says with a sigh. "I'm not sure I can take it."

I don't know what to say, so I don't say anything.

After a long moment, Riley picks up his fork and starts eating again. "So, you grew up in Granite?"

"Yes." I toy with my fork. "We don't have to make meaningless small talk now, either. I can just go."

"Don't. You said we can be friends, right? So let's give that a try."

"Friends?"

"Yeah. I like you, Lilah. I know you're my teacher for now, but that won't last forever. And I like spending time with you. I find you interesting. Besides, I can't talk about painting with any of my teammates, and I have a lot to say."

That makes me smile. "Oh, yeah? Like what?"

"Like ... like this Pop Art stuff. That's totally different from your style. But you said that Rosenquist had a big influence on you. So how do you know what your style is?"

I furrow my brow. "I don't know. No one has ever asked me that before. I guess it's about what speaks to you."

"I feel like everything speaks to me," he laughs. "I

want to try everything. Are you teaching again next semester?"

Disappointment makes my frown deepen. I never would have believed this just three weeks ago, but I love teaching. "Marty will be back in time for fall semester. Have you taken any other art classes?"

"This is my first."

"You might want to try a more specialized class. It's nice to try a little of everything, but we don't really get to delve deep into a single technique."

"Yeah," he says, rubbing the back of his neck. "I wish I could. But I've only got this year of school left."

"What will you do after?"

"That's the million dollar question," Riley says, staring off over my shoulder. "This is my last year to be eligible for the NFL draft. If I get picked up, I'll play."

I thank the waitress as she refills my coffee and busses some of Riley's plates. It gives me time to say out loud what I'm thinking. "You don't sound terribly excited about it."

He chews on his lip for a moment before he replies. "With everything that's happened in the last year, football just isn't the same. Like I said, those guys were my friends. What they did tainted the game for me."

"So why are you still playing?"

"Habit? Up until recently, football was all I ever wanted," he says with a shrug. "You want some of these fries?"

"Sure," I say, dipping one in his pile of ketchup.

"My whole family plays football," he says as I crunch into a fry. "It's football or the farm, and that's it. I never planned on doing anything else."

"What would you do, if you could do anything?"

He ponders that for a long time. "See, that's the problem. My whole life, the answer has been football. But now ... I wish I could go back and undo what happened to your friend, and find a way to guarantee that it wouldn't happen to anyone else. But I can't do that. So I've got to figure out a way to live in a new reality."

His words strike a chord deep inside me. It's my turn to touch his hand. When he looks up, I smile. "I know exactly what you mean."

CHAPTER TEN
Riley

Lilah walks back to my dorm with me where, unfortunately, the party is going harder than ever. "I somehow hoped that this would magically be over by now."

She checks her watch. "It's not even ten. I expect you've got quite a few hours to go."

"I never liked this kind of party," I say, staring up at the windows. "Too many drunk, stupid people being drunk and stupid."

"I used to like these kinds of parties."

"Used to?"

"Natalie did, and I usually had fun when she dragged me along."

"Ah." I don't have anything to say to that. "You've come to parties at Taylor Hall? I can't believe I never noticed you."

"Once or twice," she says, her eyes far away. "But binge drinking has lost its appeal for me."

"Yeah, me too. I can't believe I let Reggie talk me into this."

"This is Reggie's doing?" She surveys the laughing

people sprawled over lawn chairs in the front yard, the streamers trailing out of half the windows, the sophomore gloomily cleaning up vomit. "Well, I guess he learned one thing in college—how to throw a party."

"It's the other thing he's good at," I say. Then I have an idea. "If I got Reggie to come to every class from here on out, could he still get a passing grade from you?"

She frowns. "There's an attendance requirement. If you count getting kicked out of the first class, he's already missed too many. But I guess if he doesn't miss any others …."

"He won't," I say, with more confidence than I feel. But I need to prove to her, in some weird way, that what she thinks of football players isn't true.

"You're going to convince Reggie to come to class? How?"

"Easy," I say, grinning at her. "I'm bigger than he is."

Her face splits into a wide smile. The urge to kiss that beautiful mouth is so intense I almost—almost—forget that she doesn't want me to.

It doesn't matter that I think her reasons are weak, and that she's still mixed up over her friend's death. She said no, so no it will be.

My mind is dealing with that reality a lot better than my body. Spending an hour with her up close has me even more riled up than when I was watching her in class. Now I know how she crinkles her nose when she's thinking. Now I know how she looks licking the last bit of blueberry pie off her fork.

I'm a grown man, I can handle it. But dammit, I wish I could switch off my response to her as easily as she's turned off her response to me. Because it was here, earlier, when she saw me in that stupid grass skirt Reggie made me wear. I know when a woman wants my body. Yet she refuses to admit it, and I'm not going to force her.

"Well, I guess I'll see you on Monday," she says.

I barely stop myself from asking her to come up. Or asking to go home with her. Or asking for any way to spend a little more time with her. But I repeat to myself the words that I already knew will be my mantra—*just friends, just friends.*

"Yeah, I guess I'll see you Monday," I say aloud. "And you know, I am literally always hungry, so if you ever want to hit up Duke's again, let me know."

She stares at me for a long moment, and again I fight the urge to kiss her. Eventually—probably—this will get easier. This crazy attraction will subside. Until then, I will just have to figure out how to handle it.

"Okay, sure," she says finally. "Maybe I … maybe I have been judging you because you're a football player. I should make the effort to get to know you as a person."

"And I can pick your brain about painting. It's a win-win." I watch her straddle the bike and fasten her helmet. "Can you ride that thing in heels?"

She glances down at her gray ankle boots. "Honey, I can do anything and everything in heels."

She probably means things like walking and dancing, but the images that spiral through my mind involve much more creative positions. *Just friends, just friends.* "Uh … be careful getting home."

Lilah looks back toward the raging party in my dorm. "Be careful getting to your room. And maybe—could you maybe keep your eyes open tonight? Make sure no one is ...."

She doesn't finish the thought, but she doesn't need to. Silently, I say good-bye to the idea of heading up to my room alone and locking the door. "I'll keep my eyes open."

"Thanks," she says on an exhale. "Thanks."

Then she's riding away. And I'm going inside, to babysit a bunch of drunks.

Over the next three weeks, I try to think of Lilah as a friend, a teacher. I try to think of her as a professional, as a peer, as a pal.

None of it works. I still want to fuck her silly.

"Fuck, man. I can't wait for this class to be over."

I glance over at Reggie. With bribery, threats, and some minor violence, I have managed to do the impossible: Reggie has attended every art class. "You better not let Lilah hear that."

"Ooh, Lilah's gonna be mad," he says tauntingly, elbowing me as we walk to class. "She's got big strong Lotto wrapped around her finger."

"Shut up, dude. I told you, it's not like that."

"Yeah, okay. I believe you when you say you aren't fucking her, because if you were, you'd be a lot more relaxed."

I glare at him. "Don't talk about her that way."

"Shit, you've got it bad, bro."

"Seriously, Reggie. Leave it alone."

Reggie shrugs. "Honestly, it makes all this art shit worth it. Watching you drool over her is hilarious. It's nearly more fun than fucking with that British asshole."

"I do not drool," I say shortly, even though I know my lies are worthless. Reggie knows she better than that. "Look, she's my teacher, and we're friendly, but that's it."

"Uh-huh. Sure. Totally."

Before he can tug open the classroom door, I stop him with a hand on his shoulder and a threat in my voice. "Just shut up, do your final project, and then you're done, okay? I'll never harass you about going to class again."

When I open the door, Lilah turns to look at me. I go still, which just makes Reggie huff with silent laughter. But I can't move. The impact of seeing her never seems to lessen. Today she's wearing a leopard-print wrap dress that nips in at her waist and shows off her deep cleavage. She also has on a pair of strappy orange heels that make her legs appear a million miles long. But what stops me short is the look on her face. Like, for just a second, I caught her yearning for me.

Just friends, just friends.

With effort, I force myself to turn toward my seat. She hasn't made a single indication in the last few weeks that she's interested in me. Sometimes I think there's something—a flash in her eyes, a hitch in her breath—but she never gets close enough for me to know for sure.

We've gone back to the diner a couple of times—once when I asked her, once when she asked me. She tries to maintain a teacher-student barrier, but it's hard to stay distant when we have so much to talk about. Her life has been completely different from mine. From her stories about her grandmother, I gather that she is responsible and loyal. From the lack of stories about her parents, I get the impression that, wherever they are, they haven't been a part of her life for a long time. And from the way she's slowly opening up about Natalie, I can see she is still grieving for her friend.

It's probably a good thing she closed off the romantic side of our relationship. Otherwise, I'd be in danger of falling in love with her.

Which would be a terrible idea. As my father reminds me during his increasingly frequent phone calls, I really need to focus on football. Over the last six weeks, Coach Prescott had worked us hard. As a result, we are finally starting to play as a team. It's not like the Mustangs of old, but maybe that's a good thing. I can see now that MoFo was stuck in his ways, determined to run the team the same way every year. Coach Prescott seems more interested in discovering our talents instead of worrying about how we fit into his system.

And it's just in time. As soon as today's class is over, he'll have training camp and two final weeks to make us the best team possible. I know that, as soon as this class is over, I'll have to put aside this indulgent little fantasy and focus on football. I'm going to miss it. Almost as much as I'm going to miss seeing Lilah three times a week.

"Whatever you produce during today's class will be your final project," she says when class begins. She's wearing those black-rimmed glasses again, which never fail to drive me crazy.

"The medium and subject matter are completely up to you," she's saying as she paces. "I expect you to use the techniques you've learned in this class, but I'm more interested in seeing you represent yourselves."

Her eyes flick over to me, then skip away. "Ah ... feel free to use any materials you like. I'll be here if you have any questions, but really this project is about you. So let's get started."

Most of the class gets up and heads toward the supply cabinet, but I study my blank canvas for a few minutes. What represents me? Once upon a time, it would have been football. But that isn't enough anymore. I think about the last year, about the way the world I know has turned upside down.

Beside me, Reggie walks up to his canvas with a thick brush and a tray of red acrylic paint. Without hesitation, he slops his brush into the paint and draws a huge red circle on his canvas. "There. That represents me."

"Jesus, Reggie. Try to put a little effort into the project."

"What? I'm done."

"Reggie, come on."

"Hey, Lilah, I'm done," he shouts over the chatter in the room.

She comes over, careful not to meet my eyes. "That was fast."

Reggie shrugs casually, but his jaw is set. "Check it out. A big, bold zero—that's me."

She glances from the canvas to his face, then back to the canvas. "If you say so."

"Sweet, so I'm done then? See you suckers later," Reggie says, strutting out the door.

"Well," says Lilah with a sigh. "At least you got him to come to class."

"Yeah," I say, staring at Reggie's painting. Was that really how he saw himself? "So does he pass?"

"I suppose so," she says, turning to me with a smile. "You're a good friend."

Her smile is so sweet. But I don't want her

sweetness. I want her passion, her intensity. My hands twitch with the need to touch her. We're in a busy classroom full of students, but for a second it's as if there's no one else in the world.

"I'll be right back," I say, standing abruptly.

"Riley?" she asks uncertainly.

"Just wait," I say, jogging out the door.

I know what I'm looking for. MSU's campus is full of beautiful, well-tended trees, but there was a storm yesterday, and I noticed a white oak that lost some branches on the way to class. I know exactly which piece I want—a large, sturdy thing with one end raw where it split from the trunk.

I tote the branch back inside, where Lilah waits for me with an eyebrow raised. She just stares at the branch I'm hauling.

"Can I do something a little different for my final project?"

Her face moves from confusion to comprehension as she looks from the huge branch, to the wood wedge in my hand, to the small figurines that, by now, number nearly a dozen. "Riley … are you the one who's been leaving these little carvings?"

I shrug. "That's just for fun. But you said the final projects could be anything we want, right?"

"Sure, as long as you use a technique you've learned from this class. But, Riley, you've been hiding these things all over the classroom for nearly two months! Why?" Her lips are parted, her eyes wide.

"I like surprising you."

She huffs out a little laugh, then looks around the room at all her students and consciously steps back from me. "Um … okay, if this is what you want to do, I say go for it."

I sit down at my table, running my hands over the wood. Despite the rough appearance, the wood is supple and straight where I scrape away the bark. When I know what it needs, I make the first cut.

I'm used to working while things are going on around me, so the buzz and hum of a dozen artists at work doesn't bother me at all. Lilah peeks over my shoulder a few times, distracting me with her perfume, but she never says a word.

Around me, the class slowly empties, but my project isn't anywhere near done. Even with my hands working at record speeds, I've got hours left to turn this raw piece of wood into the work of art I can picture in my mind. As the final student hands in her project, I glance up at Lilah. It's time—past time—to turn in the piece, yet Lilah just nods at me to continue. I nod back then turn my attention back to the art taking shape under my hands. She's watching me, I can feel it. The intensity of her gaze far outpaces what I feel from an entire stadium of screaming fans, but I channel the legendary game day focus and concentrate.

I don't have any sandpaper with me, or my finer tools, but that's all right. I want the design to be crude, raw, full of emotion.

I know the final cut the moment I make it and look up. My brain is buzzing and I feel hyper-focused, yet totally flexible. I'm ready for anything to happen. Anything ... but that doesn't stop the shock registering as I realize the sun is burning orange through the atrium windows.

"What time is it?" My voice is rough from hours of silence.

Lilah looks up from where she sits at her desk,

hurriedly closing her sketchpad. "Around seven. Finished?"

Panic grips me for a moment. Did I miss afternoon drills? Then I remember and let out a whoosh of air—Coach Prescott gave us the day off from practice for finals. "Sorry I lost track of time." I'm well over an hour past the final project deadline.

"I let everyone work until they felt satisfied. You just took the longest."

Tearing my gaze away from Lilah, I study what the branch has become—a muscular male arm with fingers outstretched. "I think I'm done."

"Good," she says, standing and striding toward me. My hyper-focus narrows in on the sway of her generous hips as she walks in those towering heels. "Can I see it?"

Wordlessly, I hand it to her. This carving is totally different from what I normally do. It doesn't look anything like the delicate figurines adorning her desk. I hold my breath, waiting for her reaction.

Lilah plays her fingertips over the rough-hewn fingers. "Is this piece reaching for help, or offering it?"

"Both."

She sets it carefully on the desk. "I shouldn't pick favorites, but … Riley. This is incredible."

Pride and satisfaction swells within me, like the moment when the Mustangs score a touchdown and the stadium explodes around me. Whooping, I sweep her up in my arms, spinning in a circle.

Whittling is one thing, but I've almost always replicated something I've seen. This is different. The arm feels like a piece of me that I've managed to extract, examine, and understand. And the fact that

Lilah could see that just amplifies the exhilaration.

"Riley, stop," she says, laughing. I spin to a stop and lower her to the floor, intensely conscious of the way her body rubs against mine.

She doesn't protest. In fact, her hands are hooked behind my head, while my hands have come to rest on her hips. In the darkening classroom, her eyes seem deep and mysterious. Sad.

"What is it?" I whisper.

"I thought I was teaching you something about art," she whispers back, "broadening your horizons. But it turns out I didn't teach you anything. You already knew how to carve like this, to create something this beautiful."

I dip my head closer to hers. "That's not true. I never could have done this without you."

She looks away, tries to step back, but I hold her fast. "Lilah, without you, I never would have known what I can do. I never would have even tried before you. You make me *see* the world, instead of just exist in it. You've given me so much, in so little time. You've taught me who I want to be."

"Riley," she breathes, her eyes like stars. Then she presses her mouth to mine.

CHAPTER ELEVEN
Lilah

THE WAY THAT RILEY'S HANDS clamp on my hips is the most satisfying sensation I have ever felt. No, wait—it's the way his hands knead and spread, his gloriously talented fingers working my flesh with the same confident prowess he used on his sculpture. Every new movement becomes the most satisfying. Now it's the way his hands slip up my back, those same long fingers spread between my shoulder blades as I arch against him in pleasure.

I've denied myself for too long, and now I'm starving for him. For weeks, I've clung so tightly to the logic declaring we can't be together. Now, all those arguments are tattered and feeble in my mind. No guilt, no excuses, can withstand my raging desire. I can't seem to stop wanting this man, and now I'm going to have him.

Riley tears his mouth from mine. "Tell me to stop. If I do something you don't want—"

"Don't stop," I say, dragging his head back. "Do anything you want, except stop."

With a groan, he kisses me again—wilder this time,

nipping at my lips until I open them with a gasp. My mind shuts right off. All I can hear is the pounding of my heart; all I can think is *yes* and *please* and *more* and *finally*.

His hands roam freely over the material of my dress, learning the curves of my hips and shoulders. My fingers are tangled in his thick, soft hair, reveling in finally touching him. His smell makes my knees weak—soap and wood and skin. And the heat of him! Like being plastered against a molten volcano.

But I'm the one who turns to lava when he finally takes my breasts in his hands.

"Fucking glorious tits," he mutters as he pulls his mouth from mine so he can watch his hands as they squeezed and stroke my breasts. "So big, so soft."

I groan, letting my hands trail down his arms and over his back. So many times I've imagined feeling his muscles under his T-shirt, and now the real thing is so much better than I'd dreamed. He is so big and hard and strong, every movement sending muscle rippling under my fingers. His waist, thick with layered abs, tapered from his barrel chest only to swell again at his thick thighs.

He backs me up until my ass hits my desk, then hoists me up so I'm perched on the very edge. The last, lavender light of day fills the room as Riley steps between my spread thighs. He leans close, his mouth a whisper from mine. "Lilah. You have to tell me what you want."

"Touch me," I say, my voice a desperate whisper.

"Here?" he says, running a finger down the center of my chest. "Now?"

"Yes," I say, reckless with need. "Riley. Please. I can't wait any longer."

His mouth quirks up as he begins to loosen the tie of my wrap dress. "I think you can. You made me wait for weeks. Now it's my turn."

I groan in protest, but Riley only smiles as my dress comes loose with a tug. He hums with appreciation as he pushes the dress off my shoulders. In the soft glow of twilight, he takes me in.

My black satin bra gleams against my dark skin, showcasing the breasts he likes so much. My soft belly quivers as his gaze travels down to my spread thighs, zeroing in on the red swatch of fabric covering my pussy. "Fuck, Lilah," he breathes, and his voice is so reverent it sounds like the highest praise.

He presses my thighs even farther apart, making room for his strong hips. He coaxes my legs up over those hips until my feet—still in heels—are spurring against his ass. I drape my arms over his shoulders, feeling hungry and wanton. "I've got a real thing for how you look in a T-shirt, but it's time to get rid of this one," I say, plucking at the soft fabric.

He grins before grabbing the shirt by the hem and pulling it over his head. My hands are on him before the fabric even clears his head. *Holy fucking shit.* His body is incredible. Heavy and thick, with slabs of muscle folded over each other. I've studied the human body, and Riley's is perfection writ large.

I run my hands up his chest, flicking his hard nipples with my thumbs. He gasps as I run my hands up over his shoulders, down his massive biceps, exploring every hard ridge of muscle. Riley, meanwhile, is at work on my bra, releasing the multiple hooks of the back clasp. He drops hot kisses over my tattooed arm and shoulder, nipping at my skin as I arch against him.

When he finally frees my breasts, he takes them with greedy hands. His mouth follows, skimming wild kisses until he finds my nipple and takes it lightly between his teeth. I moan, holding his head closer as I sink my fingers into his thick hair. I'm clinging to him now, trusting that his solid strength can take my weight as I writhe against him.

When his hand covers my pussy, I throw back my head with a gasp. Something clenches inside me, needy and desperate. "Please," I manage, my voice breathy and hot.

Riley straightens, leaving my nipples wet from his mouth. His hair is tousled, his eyes wide with desire, but his teasing grin is back. "Is this what you want?" he asks, tracing a finger down my slit through my soaked panties.

"Yes," I moan, biting my lip.

He slips an arm around my back to support me and pulls me closer. "Do you want my fingers inside you? My mouth on your clit?"

The words, delivered with his flat, prairie twang, send a shock wave through me. "Yes," I sob, nearly bucking off the desk.

His thick fingers shove my thong aside and plunge inside me. He swallows my cry of shock with his mouth, his tongue mimicking the thrust and twists of his finger inside me. Then he slips a second finger in beside the first, stretching me even wider, and my body explodes.

Riley drops his head to my shoulder as I clench around his hand, coming to completion faster than I ever have before. Before the orgasm subsides, he starts pumping into me again, this time finding my clit with his thumb. I may have screamed, but in this moment I'm too focused on what is happening inside me to know. Riley is kissing me again, our mouths open and avid, my body trembling against him even as I can feel the muscles in his back tightening into rocks.

With a growl he pulls his fingers from me, and I moan in frustration. With no apparent effort, he hoists me in his arms and carries me to the nearest table, where he lays me down across its surface. He lifts my limp legs, stopping to kiss the inside of my ankle as he tugs off my stretched panties. Desperately eager, I rear up so I can push off his pants.

"Not yet," Riley says, angling his hips away from me. "I'm not done with you yet."

I moan in frustration. "It's my turn to make you come."

He chuckles, deep in his chest. "Oh, you will. I'm barely holding it together as it is." He picks up my hand and runs it over the bulge in his pants. "Can't you feel how much I want you?"

My eyes pop wide. His cock is as big as the rest of him—long and thick under my exploring fingers. But when I try to slip my hand into his pants, he moves away again.

"Soon," he says, kneeling down next to the table. "But I want you wet and open and ready, so you can take me."

I push myself up on trembling elbows as I watch him settle between my legs. His eyes flick up to mine. "I want to taste you, Lilah. I want to make you come on my tongue."

"Jesus, Riley, I never expected you would talk dirty."

He nips at my inner thigh as he massages his hands up my legs. "Haven't I already defied all your expectations?"

My laughter chokes off in my throat when he strokes my pussy with those big fingers, opening me to him. He keeps his eyes on mine as he lowers his head.

The first long lick makes me gasp. The second makes me quake. Then his fingers slip inside me as his mouth finds my clit, and I surrender to the volcano he is stoking inside me.

When the orgasm hits, it's in a wave so strong that my back arches up off the table. My legs are wrapped around Riley's shoulders, my fingers in his hair, my body undulating with passion. I ride the energy of it, struggling to sit up and tug Riley's mouth to mine. I can taste myself all over him, and it only makes me hotter. "Now, Riley, now. I need you inside me now."

Night has fallen completely, but my eyes are adjusted enough to see that Riley's eyes have gone feral with need. "I've got a condom in my gym bag."

I nod, reluctant to let him go but eager to have him back. He kicks off his shoes as he stumbles to where he's left his bag, stripping off his socks with an abandon that makes me laugh. He leaves his athletic pants in a pile and starts to shove off his boxer briefs, but stops when I call his name. "I want to do that."

My legs are still weak, but I manage to stand and saunter over to him, wearing only my heels. He has all but reduced me to a puddle, and now it's time to return the favor. "Let me touch you first," I whisper, laying my hands on his hot skin.

He holds still, the condom in one hand, as I circle him.

"Look at this body," I murmur, running my hands down his back to his muscular ass. I massage his tightly-clenched cheeks as I dash kisses over his shoulder blades. I lay my head against his strong back, running my hands around his hips. I can hear his heart pounding as I push down his boxers with one hand and take his massive cock into the other.

He hisses out a breath as I stroke him. "You're driving me crazy," he groans, arching his back to look over his shoulder at me.

I smile into his back. "You're not the only one who's been waiting for weeks. I have a lot of exploring to do."

He groans again, but holds still as I slink around his body, my hands never leaving his skin. "I thought you wanted me inside you."

"I do." In the dark, standing in the center of his naked desire, I feel bold and hungry. "But I want to taste you, too. Do you want that, Riley?"

His voice is raspy. "I don't know if I can take it."

"Why don't we find out?" I say as I sink to my knees in front of him.

When I take his cock in my mouth, he groans low and deep. He is so big, I can't take him all, but I compensate by wrapping both hands around his length. I use my tongue to stroke his sensitive head and feel him twitch in my hands.

"Nope, can't take it," he says with a gasp, pulling me to my feet. "If I let you do that much longer I'm going to lose control."

"We'll try again later," I say with a devious smile.

That's when I realize—there will be a later. There is no way that once will be enough with him. I won't be able to walk away.

Riley sits in a chair, his legs spread wide, and pulls me closer until I'm straddling his hips. "You're in

Head in the Game

control," he says as he rolls the condom over his cock. "Go as slow as you want. I don't want to hurt you."

I look down at him then—his strong body, his serious face, his generous and gentle heart. The sensation that rolls through me is more than desire, more than the helpless yearning I've been trying to ignore for weeks. It's something richer than that, sweeter, and a thousand times more addictive.

I lean down to kiss him as I settle his cock at the entrance to my pussy. Then I pull back so I can see his eyes as I sink down onto him.

Our twin moans echo in the dark room. He is big, stretching me wide, but I'm so slick that I welcome him. I slowly pump, my thighs burning as I take inch after inch. Riley buries his face in my breasts, licking and sucking at my nipples and sending jolts of sensation rocketing through me. Then he's fully inside me, so deep I can barely breathe.

Slowly, I begin to rock and swirl my hips. Riley gasps, subtly moving his hips so he feels even deeper, even bigger. Slowly, my rocking becomes rising, becomes stroking, as I steadily increase the speed until I'm thrusting against him.

I kiss him desperately, but we are both so wild by now we can barely breathe. His hands are on my ass, helping me to thrust and also spreading me wide. And he's thrusting back now, his cock touching places inside me I didn't even know exist. My thighs are shaking, my nails digging into his shoulders where I hold on for leverage, as the sensations inside me swirl, spin, then roar into a tornado.

I cry out with orgasm, but Riley won't let me stop. He braces his feet against the ground, holding me up under my thighs as he pumps into me. I cry out again with each thrust, spiraling ever higher, every part of me trembling and burning and glowing. Words are spilling from my lips, pleas and praise mix with his name, and then he slips one hand between us to rub my clit and I'm gone again, lost in the abyss of pleasure.

   Dimly, I feel Riley shudder beneath me, hear his deep groan. He freezes, gasps, and digs his fingers into my skin as he comes. Then he collapses back in the chair, and I feel absurdly triumphant that I made his strong body weak with satisfaction. I curl into him, resting my head on his shoulder with his hard cock still inside me. Right now, despite everything, I'm exactly where I want to be.

CHAPTER TWELVE
Riley

"Lilah," I murmur. I'm tracing her tattoos with my fingers, tickling her skin.

"*Hmmm?*" she replies, her head still resting on my chest.

"This feels amazing, but I'm afraid we're going to break this chair."

Her head whips up. "Oh," she cries, scrambling off of me. "I didn't—did we—"

I stand and pull her to me, not wanting to lose the connection. We both look at the chair. It was one of the standard classroom jobs, a plastic bucket seat with a C-shaped metal base. But now, that C-shape has been crushed into a U.

Lilah gapes at me. "Did we just fuck that chair into a different shape?"

"Looks like it," I say, comparing it to another chair that is discernibly less bent.

"Oh my God," she says, embarrassment tinging her voice. "What are we going to do?"

I grin at her. "I'm taking it. As a souvenir."

She frowns, suddenly professorial even though

she's totally naked. "That's school property."

"Not anymore. This is a piece of history. The chair where Lilah Stone came in my arms. Maybe I'll have it bronzed."

"Riley."

"Lilah," I say, mimicking her hands-on-hips stance. I can't help feeling goofy—I can't remember ever being this happy. "Are you going to let some unsuspecting student sit where my naked butt has been?"

I surprise a laugh out of her, which turns into a long, rolling giggle. I gather her up in my arms, loving the way her smiling face tips up at me. "I need hash browns," I say, "if I'm going to have the energy to damage more furniture with you later."

Her laugh tapers off as she lifts her hands to my chest. "Riley. We should talk."

"We will. Over hash browns."

She bites her lip, nods. She makes that lip look so soft and plush that I want to kiss her again, so I do—delighted that I *can* kiss her now, I don't have to restrict myself or pretend I don't want her. Her naked body is warm under my hands, so thrillingly close. The scent of her perfume has soaked into my skin, and I know I will still smell her later, when I'm alone. Not that I want to be alone. Not that I ever want to be without her.

When we have tracked down all of our clothes, I snag the chair with a raised eyebrow. Lilah shakes her head disbelievingly, then shrugs.

"I'll get your piece back to you in a few days," Lilah says, nodding at the wooden arm that still lay on my worktable.

"Sure. So, tell me teacher, did I earn an A?"

She pushes her hands into her mohawk, fluffing it

up as she gives me a sultry look. "Oh, I don't know. I'm going to have to see some more of your work."

I can't resist pulling her against me, covering that pouting mouth with mine. "Don't worry. I've still got plenty to show you."

Once I've ordered—easily three times as much food as Lilah—I sit back in the booth and smile. The last few times we've come here, we've both been scrupulously polite, carefully keeping our legs from brushing under the table. But now Lilah's feet are tangled with mine, her knee brushing the inside of my thigh. I no longer have to spend half the meal trying not to fantasize about the tattoo hidden under her top. I know it now; I've run my mouth over it, tasted the bright roses and darker thorns she chose to ink on her skin.

I adjust in my seat. It seems I'm still going to spend half the meal fantasizing about her naked body. Now, at least I don't have to hide it.

"So I'm thinking after this, we should go back to your place and try to break your bed."

She coughs into her coffee, then looks up at me with merriment in her eyes. "I'm sure my grandmother would love that."

"Right, your grandmother. Well, I'm not particularly attached to the bed in my dorm room."

She curls her lip. "Like I'm going to break furniture with you with a dozen football players right outside."

Valid point. "I'll put a sock on the door."

She takes a deep breath. "Can we be serious for a second?"

I reach across the table and take her hand. "What's up?"

She looks down at our joined hands. "Look, I know there's a perception that artists are all about free love and open relationships or whatever. But I'm not one of those artists."

"Okay."

"The past hour aside, I don't just jump into bed with people. Or onto chairs with people," she says with a small smile. "And we don't have to label this or make some sort of weird commitment, but—"

"Are you saying you want to go steady?" I ask, my voice amused.

"No. I mean ... no. I like you, and I'd like to see you again, but .... God, Riley, I wish you weren't a football player."

Irritation pricks at my happiness. "We're still stuck on this?"

"It's not about Natalie. Or not *just* about Natalie." Her hands flutter like birds under mine, but I don't let go. "I know what the next few months are going to be like for you—what it *has* to be like for you. If you're going to get drafted, you have to focus all your energy on being your best. You don't need the distraction of a ... whatever."

"See, I look at this another way. There's no way I could play my best unless you were my ... whatever. You make me better. I told you that before."

She looks down at the table, embarrassed. "You were talking about class."

"No, I was talking about everything. Lilah, I don't think you understand. At the end of the spring semester, I was ready to go home. I was committed to playing my last year at MSU, but I didn't have any love for the game, any heart. But over the past few weeks, I feel like I've woken up again. On the field, and in the rest of my life. And you are a big part of that."

"Is football really what you want, though?" she asks, gripping my hand. "I mean, Riley, you are so talented. The piece you created today is one thing, but all your little carvings are wonderful as well. You could sell them. You could have a career as an artist."

"Nah," I say, sitting back awkwardly. "That's just for fun."

"I know you think football is your future, but just consider it a second. I am certain that you could make a living off of your carvings. You don't have to go to the NFL—there's another option."

The concept is so foreign I immediately reject it. "No way. It's just something I do. If I told my dad I was going to carve wood for a living instead of play football, he'd laugh his ass off right before he kicked mine."

"That's how I make my living," Lilah says, going a little huffy.

"Yeah, but you're ...."

Her eyes become sharp in an instant. "I'm what?"

I stare at her for a long moment. "There is literally no way I can end that sentence without putting my foot in my mouth."

She tugs her hands from mine. "I'm what?"

I purse my lips, then decide to wing it. "You are a creative juggernaut with years of experience and a Pitkin Prize under her belt. And I'm just a country boy who whittles."

She looks at me narrowly. "You are much more than that. For example, you are an accomplished bullshitter."

I grin at her, knowing my dimple is winking. "Why, thank you."

"You know what I'm saying. The piece you carved for your final project is wonderful. That could be the start of a whole new world for you."

The project is still clear in my mind's eye. It's not so different from the hundreds of other carvings I've done over the years—it isn't the biggest, or the most difficult, or the most beautiful. But it was certainly the hardest to create. I feel like I've removed a piece of myself in its creation. I'm not sure I want to experience something that intense again. I mean what I said earlier—I never would have been able to create that piece without Lilah. "You can have it."

"Riley. No. You should keep it."

"I want it to be yours," I say, all joking gone from my voice. "You're the one who helped me see what I'm capable of."

She would have replied, but the waitress arrives with the food. Ahh, hash browns. There is no situation that can't be improved by fried potatoes. I dig in happily, then notice that Lilah is poking at her club sandwich. "What?"

She looks up at me, regret and sorrow clear in her face. "I like you, Riley. But my position hasn't changed. I don't want to be in a relationship with a football player."

I chew slowly, giving myself time to think. "Well, your position will have to change, because you're in a relationship with me, and I'm a football player. And, just to be clear, if I weren't playing football, I wouldn't be here. I have a scholarship to play, and I can't afford school without it."

"I'm not asking you to quit. Look, it's me, okay? I'm not sure I can deal with it."

"With what?"

"With being 'Lotto' Brulotte's girlfriend ... or whatever," she adds quickly. "I'm not going to make you banners or go to pep rallies or cheer for you on the sidelines."

"That's fine," I say with a shrug. "We have cheerleaders for that."

"I don't even *go* to football games."

"You don't have to," I say, though it gives me a pang to think of playing without her there.

Clearly she notices, because she asks, "Isn't that going to bother you?"

"Maybe. I don't know. What I do know is that your fries are getting cold."

She looks down at her plate, then back up at me. "Is that some sort of existential commentary on how I should live in the moment instead of worrying about the future?"

"No. It's a fact," I say, proving it by stealing a fry off her plate. "Lilah, let me make it easy for you: I'm not going to let you talk your way out of my life. If you really don't want to be my ... whatever, then you should tell me now."

She says nothing.

"So, should I take that to mean that you want to ... whatever with me?"

"Define 'whatever.'"

I want to say *spend every moment together and grow so close that we can't imagine a life apart*, but I figure that would freak her out. "For now ... hang out. Make art. Break furniture. Eat hash browns."

She smiles, and it's so beautiful it hurts.

"I think I can agree to those terms," she says, finally picking up her sandwich. Simultaneously, I feel her foot rubbing my leg. "To be honest, I can't stop thinking about how flimsy all the furniture in this diner is."

I look around, my imagination suddenly vivid. Erotic images pop into my head: propping Lilah on a stool and burying my face between her legs; laying her out on a booth and fucking her glorious tits; leaning her against the cold case so her hard nipples scrape the glass as I pound into her. When I look back at Lilah, my cock already hard, a sly smile curls on her face.

"Let's get out of here," she says, signaling the waitress. "We can pack this up to-go. We'll probably need the energy later."

"But where are we going to go?" I ask. "Your place is out, my place is out."

She chews on her lip for a moment, which is doing nothing to relax my erection.

I try to force some blood back into my brain. "My dorm room is out? I don't have a roommate."

She shakes her head. "I can't …. Don't ask me to walk through all of those guys." She looks away. "I'm just getting used to the idea of being with you. I don't think I can handle being around the whole team."

"Okay, that makes sense. Um …." I think back to what I did when I was a randy high schooler. "I have a truck."

She tilts her head, her foot tracking up to my inner thigh. "We could probably make that work."

My cock grows even harder at the words. It's going to be difficult to get out of here without making a scene. But it's not just my cock that is swelling. Looking at her, I can feel something expanding in my chest that's part pleasure, part desire. Something is happening to my heart that neither Lilah nor I are prepared for. If I'm honest, I think I'm ready for it, ready to feel this way. I just have to convince her to feel the same.

CHAPTER THIRTEEN
Riley

As the summer winds down, the MSU campus fills with students moving in for the fall semester.

But I barely notice the crowd. It feels like all that exists in this world, besides football, is this thing growing between me and Lilah. My body and Lilah's body. My heart and Lilah's heart.

I walk around in a haze, intoxicated by her even when she's not around. She's infused my entire life, making everything better. I swear, she's even affecting the team. In practice, we are finally starting to come together. West is throwing the ball well, and the team is acting like a team once again. And me? I'm faster and stronger than I've ever been. I've been bulking up, building muscle mass for years, honing my skills and working myself to the bone, but something is different now. Something has clicked, and I can't help but think that thing is Lilah. Lilah and her magic pussy. I know it's silly, but it's like she's given me super strength.

And it couldn't come at a better time. We're just minutes away from our first game of the season. All eyes are on us, watching to see if we'll choke or survive. There are still those who want Coach MoFo reinstated, who can't stop focusing on the past. But walking toward the stadium this morning, surrounded by classmates proudly sporting the Mustang blue and silver, I am so damn excited for the future.

Today should be a cake walk. Literally, that's what these games are called—cupcake games—because the athletic department purposely chooses an out-of-conference team with lesser ability to come and make us start the season with confidence. Lobbing up a nice and easy first game to kick the season off right. Sometimes I wonder about how those teams feel. Flying all the way in to be sacrificial lambs. Today, for instance, we're playing the University of Hawaii, the Rainbow Warriors. I guess with a mascot like that, they've got bigger problems than knowing they're going to lose a game.

In the locker room, Reggie sits next to me with his leg bouncing up and down. He punches a fist into his hand repeatedly, his energy spilling out of him anyway it can. As I pad up, I can't help but notice that some of the guys are holding my figurines, rubbing them like mini-Buddhas for good luck. I've been slowly leaving them in teammates' lockers before and after practice. It was partly Lilah's idea, to carve one for each player. It's been a good way to pass the time whenever I'm not drilling with the coaches or breaking furniture with Lilah. Reggie, true to his word, hasn't mentioned art class, and he even stopped some of the guys from giving me shit for carving wood when a few of the starters caught me red-handed hiding West's figurine—a compass pointing true north—in his locker. I've never been more thankful for Reggie's friendship than right then, though the distraction he chose was to yank down his own sweaty practice shorts and rub his ass all over Ben's gym bag. The arrogant new wide receiver nearly exploded with rage.

Speaking of Ben, even he is holding one right now. He's sitting in a corner—not speaking to anyone as usual—and palming his figurine. It's a little carving of an Aston Martin, because that car reminds me of James Bond and stuffy Ben Mayhew sounds a lot like the infamous 007. Ben looks up suddenly and catches me staring. He scoffs and shoves the figurine away, and I can't help but shake my head. That guy makes no sense to me. Maybe I'm too country to understand him.

Instead, I focus on Coach Prescott. He's holding his clipboard and looking over us, chewing the inside of his lip, but not saying anything. Finally, he puts a hand up and ends the idle chatter.

"Men," he says. The locker room goes silent and nervous energy pings through the room. "We've busted our asses practicing for this moment. This is the moment where we prove that we're more than a hashtag. We're more than a scandal. We're a strong tradition of excellence on the field. There's been a lot of talk during the off-season, but now the time for talk is over. Now is the time for action."

He holds his hand out toward us and we stand up together, putting our hands in the center as one unit. All together, our hands dip down and we all yell from the bottom of our stomachs, "Can't stop the stampede!" Anticipation and adrenaline flood through me, so much I'm bouncing up and down, barely holding back from sprinting out of the locker room and onto the field. With Coach in the lead, he leads us out of the locker room and toward our fate. Following a tradition started generations before us, we each slap a hand for good luck against the words painted over the door leaving the locker room: "Can't stop the stampede." The words are aged and the paint starting to chip from so many hands touching it year after year, but I swear I can feel all those other players imbuing me with strength. I'm a Mustang, dammit, and I cannot wait to show the world what that really means out on the field.

The stands are already bursting with throngs of fans. It's hot as hell, but the student section is going nuts as we take the field. As I look up and around the the full stadium, I see fans swathed in blue and silver, with half-coconut shells strung around their necks, holding signs, cheering for us. Nearly all the students are wearing their Mustang hats, a giant thing shaped like a horse's head with a long, blue manes flowing down their necks.

In this moment, there's no doubt this is where I'm meant to be. For the first time since the scandal, I feel truly at home. The green turf, the blue sky, the rowdy fans—it fills me with the simplest pleasure. I've been coming to this stadium since I was a kid, watching the games and playing with a miniature football. There is nothing *nothing* like college football. I search the crowd for Lilah, even though I told her she didn't need to come. But I can't quell the hope to see her anyway. I want to share this moment with her. The buzz in the air is irrepressible, and I *know* if she could just experience this for a second, she might see another side to football. The side I love. The camaraderie and raw energy, the anticipation and elation.

Before I know it, special teams is lined up on the field and the coconuts are clapping, slowly at first and then gaining momentum, clattering faster and faster as our kicker, Trent Richards, approaches the ball. Hawaii won the coin toss and chose to receive, so I'm on the sidelines for the first play, and I'm beside myself with jitters.

The clattering from the coconut shells—our "stampede"—reaches a deafening roar as Trent winds up and kicks. We're off, the ball soaring through the air to the end zone. Hawaii catches the ball, and it's a rush of blue and silver colliding with green and white.

Except the Hawaii player who catches the ball slips through the collision, finding space on the field to break through. My stomach drops. Blood drains from my face. There's nothing but open field in front of him, and he's off like a shot. All around, the crowd groans and screams in frustration. This can't be happening, but it is. Our men scramble to catch back up with him, but it's too late. Far too late. He's out of reach, and just like that, within the first ten seconds of the game, we're down 7-0.

"What the fuck!" Reggie bursts out at my side. His fists are clenched and a tendon in his neck is bulging. The energy he had in the locker room needs to get onto the field now, before he explodes, standing here on the sidelines. I look down the sidelines to the rest of the team. West is white as a ghost and sweating, even though we haven't even run a play yet.

With a whistle, we jog onto the field and line up. Reggie, at center, eyes the Rainbow Warriors.

"Mike 22!" he yells out, informing West and the rest of the line that Number 22 is aiming to blitz. The player is off my right shoulder. Reggie snaps the ball and I bulldoze into the guy, stopping him on his cut toward West. I've given our quarterback ample time to make a decision—throw or run—but West just holds the ball. He's scrambling backward, searching for somewhere to throw the ball, and even though I'm holding off brute of a man, even I can see Ben cutting up the field. He's tied up with a defender, but he's faster, and if West could just let the ball fly right now —*right now*—we'd have a chance to retaliate with our own touchdown.

But he sees Ben a moment too late and underthrows the ball. It drops to the field with a disappointing thud, but at least it's not intercepted. Yet all around us, I can feel the energy in the stadium waning. We're losing our fans, and that makes my heart twist. I steel my spine and jog back to the line. We can pull this off. We can show *everyone* what we're capable of.

Second down, and we're back on the line. The play call is for me to act like I'm going to block, then roll out and sprint in a straight line down the field—it's one of my secret talents as one of the best tight ends in college football. Reggie snaps the ball and barrels into the defenders coming for West, but as I juke and roll, the tackle to my left, who's supposed to pick up my defender, has gotten distracted. I don't know if he missed the play call or saw a butterfly, but he's nowhere in sight, leaving a gaping hole in our line. West, left completely vulnerable, stutters and trips over his own feet, just barely catching himself before the defense hits him hard, sending him flying backward in a brutal take down. He hits the ground hard, but at least he doesn't drop the ball.

Groans fill the stadium, echoing within my helmet and mixing with the sound of my own labored breathing. What the fuck is happening to us? I jog over to extend a hand to West, but he shakes his head and pushes himself to his feet. His eyes look a little bleary, and I honestly don't know if it's from the hit or the total breakdown of the team he is ostensibly captaining.

"You okay, West?" I shout, grabbing hold of both sides of his helmet.

"Yeah," he says distantly. He shakes his head again. "Yeah."

But he's not okay. None of us are okay. We're a damned mess on the field, and it's a mercy when the clock ticks down and we're allowed to escape back to the locker room. As I trudge into the room, I spy my own figurine—the half-finished owl I left for Lilah the first day of class—laying on the bench in front of my locker. I can't help but if my lucky charms, without Lilah nearby to give them her essence, have become hexes.

The locker room is downright depressing. No one speaks, no one even looks at each other. Heads hang, like the weight of the scoreboard is a weight on our shoulders. We're losing 21-3. How is that even possible? This was supposed to be the cupcake game. It was supposed to be a blow out. And it is. Only it's happening in the wrong direction.

Whispers and grumbling starts hissing in the silence as my teammates break into groups. Blame is being laid, discord is being sown. I'm tempted to retreat, too, but these factions aren't right.

"We need MoFo back," I hear Dwayne Sheehan mumble under his breath to Trent Richards. Trent nods his head. I can't believe he actually agrees with this, as if it's Prescott's fault his punt was returned for a touchdown. Guys are slumped on the benches, others are pacing. Ben has his head in his locker like he's looking for something, Reggie's got his head rested against his locker, looking up at the ceiling with his jaw clenched. We're acting just like we were playing on the field—broken, defeated, individuals. Not a team. Hell, we played like we'd never been on a team in our entire lives.

I jolt up off the bench and stand tall.

"We don't need MoFo back," I say suddenly. A few guys laugh incredulously, a few more curse at me. But I can't sit back down, not until I've said my piece. "We don't need Jeremy Hudson back. We had a star coach and a star quarterback, and we won games. But I'd rather have self-respect than a championship title. And that's something I can't have under Coach MoFo. I don't feel a lot of pride around the way we're playing right now, but I'm proud that we're still here. We lost our coach. We lost some of our best players. And we're losing this game, but we are not losers."

The locker room is silent, so silent I can hear my blood pumping in my ears. I stare at my teammates in turn and continue. "Every day that we get up and sweat and bleed onto that field trying to build back a dynasty, we're proving that we have the pride to be more than what everyone expects of us. We can be better than what's expected. We *are* better. Coach Prescott has made me faster and stronger than I've ever been. I don't want to sulk here for the next twenty minutes and feel sorry for myself. I want to prove that we're more than Coach MoFo. Both on and off the field. I want to win, but more than winning, I want to feel proud of who we are."

Every eye in the room is on me, and I for a second I think I'm going to get booed out of the locker room, but then West nods his head and Reggie pounds his fist on his chest.

"Lotto's right," West says, standing next to me. "We're acting like we've already lost this game. Let's get out there and play like we know we're going to win."

That gets some cheers. The guys are perked up. The dirt and grass stains transform: What once signaled a sad pummeling now looks like a hard-fought game that's not over yet.

All too soon, we're back on the field, but my confidence is renewed.

The second half feels like a new game. We're playing better. It's not perfect, but don't look like a mess of guys who all speak different languages. We manage to hold off the Warriors and restrict them to the 21 points they had scored by halftime. We don't quite come back enough to win the game, but we score two touchdowns to end the game 21-17.

We lost the game, and with this first game, we've probably lost any hope of a championship. Even if we win every other game for the rest of the season, we'll need every other team to have two losses on their record. Losing to the University of Hawaii will haunt us to the bitter end. But here's the thing: We lost, but we played our asses off. We lost on our own terms. For as strange as it feels to say, we *earned* a defeat, and I can't help but feel we'll use it to grow stronger.

But my dad, I'm sure, will spend his every waking hour trying to build a time machine so he can talk me into going into last year's draft. When I turn on my phone, I have six missed calls from him, and none from Lilah. It's the zero missed calls from Lilah that stings the most.

I'm exhausted, and not just physically. I feel emotionally wrung out from the despair of the first half and the futile hope of the second half. All I want now is to crawl into bed and feel Lilah's soft skin on mine. But I know better than to ask her to come to my dorm. I'll just have to settle for dreaming about her instead.

CHAPTER FOURTEEN
Lilah

The canvas in front of me is empty. My colors are mixed, the canvas is prepped. But I stand there in the second-story converted studio, palette in hand, and can't make myself lay down that first brush stroke.

For as long as I can remember, landscapes have spoken to me. Growing up in the mountains helps, because everywhere you look there's a stunning vista. But my love of landscapes goes far beyond that. I paint cities, too, and the plains, and the ocean. There's something about that spot where the sky meets the ground that I can't stop trying to capture, that never ceases to fascinate me.

At least, it used to. I would see something and be driven to paint it, to capture how I felt in that moment, capture how the generations who have come before me may have felt standing in that exact same spot. The need to paint would tug at me until I satisfied it, until I managed to get what I felt onto a canvas. Art was a burning coal inside me, always ready to be fanned into flame.

Or that's how it used to be.

With a defeated sigh, I step back from the canvas. I woke early this morning into the most glorious pink dawn spreading through the sky. The clouds were fuchsia against a cerulean blue, and I felt something rise inside me that has been dormant for months. I needed that sky; I needed to learn its secrets.

Now, hours later, I'm nowhere. I have already tried and abandoned several sketches, disappointed with what I'm creating. Everything seems prosaic, pedestrian, no more vibrant than a Bob Ross painting. Not that I'm hating on Bob Ross, but I'm better than that. Or, at least, I was once.

I set my palette down and check my phone. My heart bounces when I see a text from Riley. *Class got out early. Want to hang out?*

It came in twenty minutes ago. I really should keep working, but I can't stand to keep staring at the blank canvas feeling nothing. I hurriedly text him back. *Sure. What do you want to do?*

While I wait for him to text back, I make a cup of tea and pad out onto the second story porch. I have fond memories of sitting out here with my grandmother when I was a little girl, having tea parties and fashion shows. But today, with Gamma out getting her nails done and going to the store, I have the entire house to myself. I have to admit, I'm not sure what to do with myself with all this quiet.

I glance back at my phone. Riley still hasn't texted back. I tell myself that I'm not the sort of girl who's desperate for attention, even as I stare at my phone, willing him to get back to me.

It has been a few weeks since the end of the summer semester, the night Riley and I got together for the first time. We have seen each other as often as his class and practice schedule allows, but it still doesn't seem like enough. Last week, we had to go nearly four full days without seeing each other. When he finally had a break in his schedule, we'd gone after each other like wild animals.

I grin into my tea, thinking about it. Having sex with Riley ... it's like winning the lottery and the Olympics and an Oscar all at once. The things he does to my body make me feel kinky and adventurous, but also totally safe and cherished. And every single inch of him makes me wild. I never tire of exploring his muscular frame.

And it isn't all sex. Well, I won't lie, it's mostly sex, but in between bouts of sweaty orgasms we cuddle and laugh. We spend many nights driving up into the mountains, talking about our lives and our pasts until we find a spot we can park his truck and tear into each other. I've been here before, this giddy early stage of a relationship when everything is exciting and new. But something about Riley feels deeper, stronger than that.

That thought makes a little trickle of fear drip through me. Riley's stuck to his word—he doesn't seem to care that I didn't attend his first game of the season, though after how bummed he seemed, I kind of wish I would have gone. Kind of. He has barely mentioned the game, though he does talk about practice and the guys on his team. Still, when I think about what football means to him—what it means to his future—I wonder whether I can deal with it in the long term.

But I don't want to think about the long term. I want to think about right now ... and why Riley hasn't texted me back.

I'm so busy staring at my phone I almost don't notice when his truck pulls up to the house. If my heart bounced when I saw his text earlier, it positively leaps to see him climbing out of the cab of his truck. He looks up at me, and from the expression on his face, his heart is leaping just as much as mine.

"Well, hey there, Juliet."

"Does that make you Romeo?" I ask, leaning over the railing and grinning like a fool.

"Don't you think I qualify?"

"Hmm, I don't know," I tease, shaking my head.

He reaches back into his truck and grabs something off the seat. "How about now?" he says, offering me a bouquet of red roses.

It's cheesy, but my heart swells. "You brought me flowers?"

He nods, evidently pleased with himself and my reaction. "Do I need to climb the balcony for a kiss?"

"You could. Or you could use the stairs," I say, gesturing to the back of the house.

I dash romantic tears from my eyes as he bounds up the stairs, his smile wide, and I do the only thing I can think of—I throw open my arms to him.

He lifts me into a kiss, holding me tight. His mouth is familiar by now, but that doesn't make it any less exciting. Beneath the passion, there's happiness and affection. I can feel his heart pounding in the same rhythm as my own, smell the roses where he grips them against my back. If I could paint this moment, it would be all bright colors and big bursting rays of joy.

He finally breaks the kiss, only to start backing me through the doorway into the studio. "I missed you."

"You saw me yesterday."

"Too long," he says, then picks up his head and

looks around. "Is this where you paint?"

The space is slant-roofed and small, made smaller by the stack of big canvases propped against the wall. The wood floors around my easel are splattered with long-dried oil paint, and my supply closet stands open in the corner. I still have music playing faintly from my blue tooth speakers. A door leads to a second studio that we rent out, but it's been vacant the last few months since the jewelry maker moved to New York.

A smile splits Riley's face when he sees all the carvings he's given me lined up on the windowsill. Every time I see him, he manages to slip another one into my pocket or purse without me noticing. I keep his sculpture from the final project in my bedroom, but I like having all the whimsical little carvings here. It sort of feels like they're cheering me on. Though maybe they need to cheer a bit louder.

Riley turns to the canvases and starts flipping through them. "They're all blank," I say, before he can ask.

"Where's your finished work?"

I shrug, pretending to be more casual than I am. "Nothing's working."

"It will," he says, with an easy faith I don't reciprocate.

Wanting to change the subject, I say, "You got out of class early?"

He nods. "Practice isn't until five, so I figured I'd stop by and see you."

"How's practice going?" I ask, more interested in redirecting the conversation away from my art—or lack thereof—than I actually am in the subject.

"Good. Coach has us doing this new drill with

exercise balls that is killing my quads. It's weird—I did the same drills with MoFo year after year. It was boring, but I knew it worked because we were winning games. Now Coach Prescott has us doing all this crazy shit, and it's way more interesting, but I don't know if any of it is going to matter. After last week ...," Riley trails off and hooks a hand behind his neck. "Even if we get our act together, we'll have to be basically perfect to contend for the National Championship."

He catches himself. "Sorry, you don't want to talk about this stuff. I'm sorry painting isn't going well. Maybe you need to change something up. Use a different medium, or try to work somewhere else."

"Maybe," I say with a noncommittal sigh. "Really, the only thing that's been working for me lately is sketching."

"Oh, yeah? Can I see something you've been working on?"

I usually don't show people my sketches, but I finished one of Gamma last night that actually made me proud. After a moment's hesitation, I grab the battered sketchbook off the top of the supply cabinet and flip to the charcoal sketch.

Riley peers at the page over my shoulder. "Is that your grandmother?"

I nod. I captured her sitting in her favorite chair as she worked on a sudoku puzzle and sang along with Aretha on the radio. Riley's arm slips around me as he studies it. "She looks like you."

"A little."

"Does your mom look the same too?"

I tense. "I guess. I haven't seen her in a really long time."

Riley makes a little noise of acknowledgment and sympathy. I haven't told him much about my mom. Not that there's much to tell. She left, so what? I think her absence hurt Gamma more than it did me.

Riley gently pulls the sketchbook from my grasp to look closer. "I love this. I feel like I can almost hear her voice."

"It's rough," I say, though I am pleased.

"Still," he says, flipping backward in the sketchpad.

Fear grips my throat, and I can barely choke out, "No, wait, don't!"

But it's too late. He's found one of the sketches I did of his face.

I first sketched him the day he kissed me, the day I told him about Natalie and that I wanted to be friends. And I'd kept up the habit as the weeks went on. At first, it was an outlet for my desire. I thought the impulse would fade after we started sleeping together. But if anything, I draw him more now. I *know* him more now; I have so many more memories to capture.

In the sketch he's now staring at, I'd tried to draw him in the moment just before his dimple winked, when his eyes were smiling but his mouth hadn't quite caught up. It still wasn't exactly right. There's something about his eyes that I'm not seeing, that I can't interpret.

"You drew me?"

When I flick my gaze up to Riley, he looks thunderstruck.

"It's not, like, a freaky stalker thing," I say quickly. I have to press a hand to my cheeks. My God, they're burning hot with embarrassment. "You have an interesting face, and I've been looking at it a lot."

"You drew me," he says again, and I can hear something under the shock ... something almost like awe. He stares at the sketch again. "I'm not this handsome."

"Yes, you are."

The naked emotion on his face makes my heart swell painfully in my chest, like it's trying to escape. He puts the sketchbook down and frames my face with his hands. "You see me," he says thickly. "And I see you."

This time when he kisses me, my heart rate slows. Time itself slows, flowing like hot, sweet honey. Emotion is pouring out of Riley, something deep and nameless that fills me to bursting with longing. To be like this forever; to never have to move past this moment. This moment when I think that Riley is falling in love with me.

He pulls away after a long moment and buries his face in my neck. Though it's muffled, against my skin, I can hear him say "thank you."

"There are more," I admit. I pick up the sketchbook without leaving his arms. Moments ago I was nervous about showing him, but now I can't help myself.

He takes the book from me and flips through it. "Is this from class?"

I'd drawn him sitting in his chair, studying a slide of a painting with his head cocked. "Yeah."

"And what about this?" he asks, his voice going deeper.

I see the sketch he's referring to and feel heat creep up my cheeks once again. "Um. Yeah. That one is more ...."

"Pornographic?" he supplies.

"It's just a figure study," I say sheepishly, trying not

to remember how lovingly I'd imagined his body as I drew it. "I hadn't even seen you naked when I sketched this."

Now his warm look turns downright devious. "You were thinking about me naked?"

"Duh," I say, earning a chuckle in response.

"And you're doing these from memory?"

"I didn't think you were the type to sit for a portrait."

"Normally, no, but you for you …." He flips to a blank page and sets my sketchbook on the easel. Then he slowly eases off his shirt, making my mouth go dry. "I'd be willing to give modeling a try."

CHAPTER FIFTEEN
Riley

LILAH'S EYES TRACK DOWN MY torso in a way that makes every moment in the gym worth it. Now that we have practice nearly every day on top of mornings in the weight room, I know my body is looking lean and hard with muscle. I *want* her to get pleasure looking at my body the same way I feel when I gaze at her sensual form.

My cock, always at half-mast when she's around, raises up as she traces my muscles with her eyes. *In for a penny*, I think, then shove my pants to the floor. My arousal is obvious under my boxer briefs, and I harden even further when Lilah's eyes latch on to my bulge.

She licks her lips. "Maybe we should skip the modeling session."

"Nope," I say, though I desperately want to be inside of her. "I'm curious to see what you can do. Where do you want me?"

"I don't do portraits."

"Yes, you do," I say, gesturing at her sketchbook. "Besides, this isn't work. This is just you and me.

Now," I say, giving her some cheesy body-builder moves, "how should I pose for you?"

She laughs, shaking her head. I can almost see the moment when she decides to do it. "Hang on."

She scampers out of the studio for a moment, then comes back dragging a chair from the front balcony. "Over here, by the window. Just sit. Casually," she says, arranging my limbs. "Good. Good. Tilt your head ... there."

She steps back to admire me. She had posed me comfortably, with legs spread and one arm hooked on the back of the chair. "How's that?" she asks, scrutinizing my position.

"Fine. Just one thing," I say, reaching out one arm and pulling her in for a kiss.

We're both turned on, so it doesn't take much for the kiss to turn incendiary. But when she starts to straddle me, I push her back. "Draw me," I say, my voice hoarse with need. "I want you to draw me first."

I'm not sure why the idea fascinates me so much. I'm proud of my body, though I'm not much of a show-off. But I want to see what Lilah looks like while she draws. I want to see what she looks like when she lets her guard down. I want to see what she sees in me.

Even though I've talked with her, laughed with her, and fucked her in every way my dirty mind can imagine, it still isn't enough. I still feel like she's holding back. There are places in her where we don't go. She won't talk about her mom and barely talks about Natalie. When I talk about football, I can feel her attention wandering.

I want to tell her that I feel like I'm entering a new phase in my football career, spurred by Coach

Prescott and this new version of the Mustangs. I'm realizing all over again how much I love the game. We still aren't playing perfectly, but I can feel the potential of our team simmering under the surface. The rape scandal is the past; now we have a chance to rewrite our future.

But Lilah can't, or won't, understand that. She's stuck in the past, so certain that nothing about the Mustangs has changed.

But my body ... that has her full attention. She is completely into my body, and how I can make hers feel. When we have sex, I love watching as her eyes darken with arousal, then go blind with pleasure. She is so responsive, as hungry and desperate as all my fantasies. It's not enough, though—I want her in every part of my life, I want her in my future. But if sex is the way to get her there, then so be it.

Sitting here now, I notice that her hands shake a bit as she picks up the pencil and approaches her sketchpad. I adjust slightly, tensing my ab muscles, but never take my eyes off of her. Over the next half-hour, I get an education.

I sometimes use models or pictures when I'm carving, to make sure I get the details right. But I've never been as focused, as observant, as Lilah is in that thirty minutes. Her hand moves quickly, though she barely glances at the drawing. Instead, her eyes consume me. I can all but feel the heat of her gaze as she contours my muscles, absorbing every inch of my frame.

Every part of me is subject to her gaze. I become aware of my ankles, my thighs, my ribs. I know she's memorizing each part of me, making it part of her. And her eyes. They're so intense, so focused. I thought I would see her without her guard up, but it was me who's being stripped, heart laid bare.

While she works, I watch her in turn. She's wearing what I'm sure she considers casual work clothes—black leggings and a silky sleeveless blouse that's already well-spattered with paint. She's barefoot, but a pair of high-heeled sandals are sitting by the door. The more I get to know her body, the more I want it. I brought her roses because the petals remind me of her skin—smooth, fragrant, lush. My mouth is dry, my heart racing, my cock aching. But still, I only watch.

Then, all too soon and yet not soon enough, she's finished. I can see it in the way her shoulders settle, her eyes clear. She sets down her pencil, steps back. Then turns the easel toward me.

She's drawn me in quick lines, somehow infusing power and movement into my relaxed pose. Every muscle is lovingly detailed, but she put the most of her work into my face. My desire is there, but also a natural confidence that I don't always feel.

"What do you think?" she says, as I stand up from my chair.

In answer, I haul her body against mine, kissing her with a desperate hunger. Knowing that she saw me like that—strong, sexy, certain—makes me mad with desire. She's on her toes, plastered against me, but it's not enough, not nearly close enough.

I pick her up under her thighs, loving the way she moans, and take two staggering steps until I have her pressed against the wall. I grind my cock against her soft leggings, feeling the heat of her through layers of fabric, as she runs her hands and mouth over as much of my torso as she can reach. I find the waistband of her leggings and plunge my hands underneath her ample ass.

She arches into me, moaning, then arrows her hands straight down the center of my torso. Impatiently, she shoves my boxer briefs down, freeing my straining cock. The purring sound that whispers out of her is enough to make my muscles shake, even before she wraps both hands around me and begins to stroke.

I press her against the wall, trapping her hands. "Why are you wearing so many clothes?" I pant, trying and failing to shove her leggings off. The heat of her pussy is so close to my fingertips. I don't wait for an answer, just drop her to her feet and strip her pants to the ankles in one move.

She's not wearing underwear. I can smell her arousal—the sweetest scent I've ever encountered. Hungry for her, I don't wait until she has her feet clear of the pants before I claim her with my mouth.

Feeling her buck and clutch at my head has me smiling into her pussy. I settle on my knees and lift one of her legs over my shoulder. I want full access, so my tongue can reach the core of her. I look up to see her fondling her own breasts, half out of that silky shirt, as she throws back her head in ecstasy.

I add fingers to what my tongue is doing and drive her, drive her, drive her, until her knees give out. She is almost incoherent as she collapses into me, her limbs boneless with pleasure. I know her now—I know I can make her come until she's brainless, and still her body will stir for me. And I need her, need to be inside her. I need her to take me in, all of me.

I leave her for only a moment, so I can find one of the condoms I've started carrying in bulk. When I turn back, she's sitting up against the wall, still wearing her shirt, watching me as she teases her fingers over her wet, open pussy. She bites her lip as she watches me roll the condom down my length, circling her clit with the tip of one finger. Any blood that was left in my brain flows right to my cock. "Yes," I say hoarsely. "Make yourself come for me."

   She gasps, but doesn't stop. I stand over her, stroking my throbbing cock, as I watch her pleasure herself. Her eyes never leave my face, and I revel in the desire she can so plainly see there. The fingers of one hand twirl and plunge while she pinches her nipple through her shirt. When she comes, her eyes fluttering back in her head while she utters a soft moan. It's the most erotic thing I've ever seen in my life.

   I fall to my knees and kiss her as I hurriedly strip the rest of her clothes off. When she's naked, I lay back and pull her on top of me. It's broad daylight. The sunlight sparkling through the window brings out the dark sheen of her skin, and I can't help but take her generous breasts in my hands as she braces herself over me.

   She takes all of me in one long stroke, which makes me groan with feverish pleasure. So hot, so tight, so fucking wet. Instead of pumping against me, she leans back as if she's posing and licks her fingertip. Then, her eyes on mine, she strokes her clit while I'm inside her until I feel her clench with orgasm.

   I'm beyond thought, beyond waiting. I'm always careful to be gentle with her, but she has driven me beyond reason. I flip her over, heedless of her back on the hard floor, and take one of her nipples between my teeth as I drive myself into her. She screams, but it's not in pain—she locks her legs and arms around me, trying to drive my cock even deeper. I lift her hips higher, my hands tight as a vise as I angle her so I can thrust into her even harder.

Her arms fall to her sides, grasping wildly for purchase on the wood floor. Her eyes are wide, wild, her lips parted as she gasps and moans. I'm hammering into her now, no thought in my head other than the primal need to take us both over the edge into madness. When I can't wait any longer, I kiss her, our mouths mating as closely as our bodies. Then the world goes white.

CHAPTER SIXTEEN
Lilah

Riley lies on top of me, pressing me into the warm, wood floor. I welcome his weight. Who needs to breathe?

He's nuzzling his face into the side of my head, where a thick fuzz is starting to grow. I have been contemplating shaving it again, since I'm enjoying my mohawk. But with Riley rubbing his face against my stubble, I'm suddenly inspired to carve some geometric patterns into my hair instead. And why not? Riley likes my mohawk, my tattoos ... my everything.

I had assumed, because he's a football player, that he would be a clean-cut guy into clean-cut girls. He not—he's into me. Maybe, if he gets more of a taste of my artistic world, he'll be into that too. He's so talented, and he's wasting it for that stupid game. If I could only prove to him that art is an option too ....

With a groan, he rolls off of me, but pulls me with him until I'm sprawled across his chest. I bury my nose in his neck, loving the way he smells. I love his body, and his sweetness, and his sense of humor. I know myself well enough to be sure I'm falling for him hard, and I've almost given up trying to stop it.

"Somebody's honking," he says, his voice thick.

I jerk my head up so fast I nearly get whiplash. "Gamma!" I say, scrambling to my feet and beginning the hunt for my clothes. "She's back from the store. I told her to honk so I could help her with the groceries."

"Cool. Can I meet her?"

I look at him, sprawled naked on the floor of my tiny studio, his cock still huge even though it's limp. "Not like that."

He grins, his dimple popping, as he levers himself off the floor. He gets rid of the condom and somehow manages to dress himself before I do. Just a moment ago, I was luxuriating in post-coital satisfaction; now I feel hot and harried and nervous. "Where the hell is my bra?"

Riley dangles it from one finger. "Come and get it."

"This isn't funny," I huff, grabbing it from his hand. My fingers fumble with the bra, like I haven't been wearing one for a decade.

"You don't have my view," he says, watching me wrestle my boobs into the cups.

"My grandma is waiting," I say, just as my words are punctuated by two quick beeps.

I throw on my shirt and am still buttoning it as I run for the door, when Riley stops me.

"Hang on, you have something on your face."

"What?" I ask, patting my cheeks.

He approaches, then bends down to give me a quick kiss. "There. Got it."

My heart swells even as I roll my eyes. "Try not to look so ... satisfied."

"Oh, but I am," Riley says as he follows me out of the studio. "At least, for now."

The promise in his words sends a shudder through me. The man is turning me into a sex addict.

I clatter down the outside stairs and wave to Gamma, who has apparently decided not to wait for me. "I'll get it, I'll get it," I call, worried I'll see strain on my grandmother's face.

"I got it already," Gamma says, hoisting a recyclable bag out of the trunk of her car. Though I feel heat rise on my cheeks from the double meaning.

"You should have waited for me," I scold, taking the bag from her. She's a little red—is she overheated? "Go on in the house, I'll take care of this."

She tugs the bag back from me. "I'm not an invalid, Lilah. I can carry some groceries twenty feet to the kitchen."

"Yeah, but you don't have to." The memory of her heart attack tugs at my conscious, all the fear of that moment coming back.

"I want to."

"Let me do it," I implore.

"No," says a deep voice beside me. "Let me do it."

In my panic, I have somehow forgotten Riley. And also somehow forgotten that this is the first time he's meeting my grandmother. Belatedly, I remember my manners. "Gamma, this is Riley Brulotte. Riley, this is my grandmother."

"Pleasure to meet you, ma'am," Riley says, and I can almost hear his dimple winking. "I'm a friend of Lilah's. And, an expert grocery carrier," he says, graciously slipping the bag from her grip.

My grandmother looks back and forth between us. "A friend of Lilah's?"

"Actually, ma'am, she was my teacher this past semester. I was so impressed with her talent and natural teaching ability, I basically begged her to start hanging out with me."

"Cool it, suck-up," I mutter. But my grandmother is already puffing up with the chance to talk about her favorite subject—me.

"Did you know she was painting when she was five? I mean, all kids are painting at that age, but Lilah's talent was always above and beyond."

"Is that so?" Riley asks, reaching into the truck for more groceries. "That's about the time I started playing football."

"I was going to say, a big boy like you—you must be a Mustang." She shoots me an odd look—she's heard me rant about football players more times in the last six months than I can count. "You boys going to make us proud this year?"

"I sure hope so," Riley says, darkness flickering over his face for a moment. "It's been a long climb, but we're giving it everything we've got."

Gamma arches an eyebrow. "The way the girls were talking in the salon this morning, it doesn't seem as though that's going to be enough."

Riley pauses, then says smoothly, "We're a lot more than we look on the field, ma'am. We just need a little more time to prove it."

My grandmother eyes him for a long moment. Whatever she sees in Riley must satisfy her, because her face relaxes into a smile. "Come on inside, and I'll get you something cold to drink."

"I'd love some milk," Riley says, gathering the rest of the groceries in his huge hands.

And just like that, they're fast friends. Gamma

starts teasing him about putting him to work, and Riley replies with a story about carrying some farm animal that has her laughing in minutes. I follow them inside, feeling oddly excluded. Why hasn't Riley told *me* that story? He's hardly mentioned his life back home. Does he think I won't care about where he came from?

Does he care about where I came from?

I push that thought aside. I came from right here, I remind myself. My good-for-nothing mother may have birthed me, but my grandmother created me. She's the one person on earth I can count on, no matter what.

And she is currently showing Riley through the house. Honestly, it's freaking me out to have him here. It feels too real, like suddenly my life is in acrylics when I'd gotten used to watercolors. There's a football player in my house. Riley "Lotto" Brulotte ... in my house ... charming my grandmother. How did my life get here?

I've always introduced Gamma to the guys I'm seeing. But Riley, I haven't even mentioned. Until today, I haven't even let him into the house. And that's because he's a football player.

The thought makes me feel sick with shame. If he were just any student, or a fellow artist, or basically *anyone* else, I would feel much more comfortable bringing him into my life. Then there wouldn't be all this baggage—Natalie, the team, our different lifestyles.

"Here's the picture I wanted to show you," Gamma says, pulling me from my increasingly sour reverie. I can only watch in horror as she pushes open my bedroom door and ushers Riley into my cluttered room. She plucks a framed photo from amidst the chaos of my vanity table. "Isn't that just the cutest thing?"

Riley holds the photo, smiling. I know what it is without looking. Gamma kneeling next to a ten-year-old me, her arm around my shoulder as I brace a canvas almost as big as I am. My gap-toothed grin is just as bright as the third-place ribbon from a local contest affixed to the painting.

"This is great," he says, his words warm. "Is this painting around somewhere?"

"I sold it," I say abruptly. Riley looks up and met my eyes.

"Lilah insists on selling everything," my grandmother says, her disapproval clear. "Of course I'm glad that pretty much any gallery in the state will sell her work, but I'd like to keep some of it with us."

"That's all well and good, but we've got bills to pay," I remind her. "I'm not so precious about my work that I won't make a living."

Riley's eyes are still on mine. "You've sold every painting you've ever done?"

I shrug. "Once I'm finished, that's it. Keeping it around won't make the work any better."

Riley's eye is drawn to his sculpture, displayed on a shelf in the corner. "But you'll keep a piece someone else made?"

"Inspiration," I say, catching a pleased flush run up his neck.

My grandmother notices the rough wooden carving of the reaching arm for the first time. "Lilah, this is wonderful. Where did it come from?"

"Riley made it." If he were an artist, I realize, I would be telling anyone who would listen all about him. About his talent—about our relationship. It would be so much easier to explain. Instead, I'm falling in love with a football player, and I can barely explain it to myself.

"Riley! Well. I didn't realize you were so multi-talented. What a wonderful thing for the two of you to have in common." Gamma, who obviously hasn't bought the whole "friend" thing, beams at me. "Aren't you a catch. Polite, charming ...," Gamma grins wickedly and glances at me. "And so strong."

Oh, Christ. I can tell from the look on Gamma's face that she is all but planning our wedding. I jump in. "I believe you promised this polite, charming, strong man some milk," I say, arching a look at Riley.

"Oh, yes, of course. I baked some chai spice cake last night, as well," she says, pulling the picture from his hand and setting it back on my vanity. She pauses, waiting for Riley to offer his arm, which he does. I swear, I don't know who's buttering up whom right now. Gamma smiles so wide she's nearly glowing. "And I want you to tell me all about that new coach. The pictures in the paper make him look just like Denzel Washington."

Riley stifles a laugh. "Well, I don't know about that, ma'am," he replies, his country charm in full force. "But he's sure working us hard."

As my grandma leads him back to the kitchen, I pause, my eyes on Riley's wood carving and my mind churning. If I can prove to Riley that he can make money from his carvings, maybe he won't care so much about football. And then, maybe, we can find a way to make "whatever" into something real.

Gamma was all smiles with Riley a few days ago, but

there are deep frown lines cupping her mouth today.

"Well, Lilah," she says, sitting at the kitchen table surrounded by papers and bills. "I don't see any way around it. I'm going to have to sell you to the gypsies to make ends meet."

My grandmother delivers the old joke in perfect deadpan. It's never made me laugh, but she keeps trying.

"Gamma, be serious. If we don't rent that empty studio, we'll be a couple hundred dollars short next month." I look helplessly at the bills spread across the table.

"Oh, we'll get someone soon. I put up an ad last week," she says, getting up to refill our coffees.

"It could be months before we rent the space." It has occurred to me that Riley might want a studio space, but not until the end of the football season. Not to mention that I would be violating a certain proverb about mixing business with pleasure.

The words "pleasure" and "Riley" are enough to spark memories. We went to the movies last night, but hadn't paid any attention whatsoever to the film. The mere thought of him was enough to make a sly grin break across my face. The things he had done to my body ... well, I shouldn't think about them in front of my grandmother.

With a bit of effort, I force my thoughts back to my impending financial ruin. Even with the money I've made from teaching, there still isn't enough. "I'm so sorry, Gamma. I always assumed that I would keep selling paintings, which would mean there would always be money, but—"

"Oh, baby girl, hush," she says, setting coffee in front of me. It's doctored exactly how I like it. "Your creativity isn't a cash cow to be milked. When you're ready, you'll paint again."

"What if I don't?"

Gamma shrugs as if I hadn't just revealed my deepest fear. "Then I'll get a job."

"You know you can't do that," I protest. "With your heart, we can't take any risks."

Gamma settles into her chair with a little groan. "I've been getting better. Even the doctor says so."

"Still." I'll never forget how scary it was, waiting in the hospital for someone to come tell me that my only family was dead. "I would rather you focus on getting better."

"Lilah, I've been focusing on getting better for three years. I've lost weight, I'm eating healthier, and I'm taking my medications … I've even been doing yoga. I think it's time I got a job."

"You're not going back to the restaurant." Gamma had worked at a local steakhouse for nearly twenty years before the heart attack.

Gamma levels a look at me. No one tells that woman what to do. But after a moment, she sighs. "No, you're right." She fiddles with the spoon sitting in her coffee. "I've been thinking I would get my accounting degree online."

I choke out a laugh. "Accounting?"

"I did the books at the restaurant for years," she says defensively.

"Really? Why didn't I know that?"

"I don't tell you every little thing, my girl. Old Mr. Harold used to bang his head against the wall trying to figure them out, so I took over," she says with a little smile. "And I've looked into it. My friend Gloria at the salon did her degree online and works from home now."

"Well ...," I say slowly, mulling over everything in my head. For three years now, I've looked after my grandmother, worried about her. It's not so easy to just stop.

"I'm not looking for permission, Lilah."

Surprise has me sitting back in my chair. "Okay. Okay." I'm still not so sure about this.

"Don't worry so much, Lilah." Gamma stacks the bills into a neat pile, like that'll get them paid on time.

A sigh escapes me. "You always say that to me, but you never tell me how I'm just supposed to shut it off."

"My darling girl. You don't shut it off, you learn to live with it," Gamma says with a sigh. "I still worry about your mother every day."

My chin pokes out. "She doesn't deserve one second of your attention."

"I'll stop worrying about her, if you stop worrying about me."

The thought of Gamma wasting her energy worrying about my deadbeat mother rankles. But I have to admit that I couldn't just switch off my love and worry about my grandmother, so I guess I can understand what she's saying.

"Well, now, what is this?"

Gamma's voice catches my attention. She's bending over to pick up a slip of paper that evidently fell out of the stacks of bills. I recognize it in an instant: the sketch I'd done of Riley earlier while trying to concentrate on the bills. Clearly, I can't get the man out of my head. That's a whole other set of worries.

Gamma sits back and holds up the paper. "You captured him, that's for sure." She looks at me with a twinkle in her eyes. "He's a cutie. You don't often draw faces."

"No," I admit. Though I'd drawn Riley half a dozen times now. I keep trying to capture this look in his eyes that makes me feel scared and safe all at once. "He's ... special."

My grandmother hums. "How are things going with him?"

"We're not dating," I say quickly, wanting to keep her from fantasizing about a future that I'm not sure Riley and I can have. "We're just ... whatever."

She fixes me with her sharp gaze. "You're seeing him."

"I guess. I don't know. We haven't labeled it."

"Young people are idiots," she says with a sigh. "Why is it such a big deal to admit that you like someone?"

"It's not. I do. I do like him, I mean. I don't know." I blow out a breath. "It's complicated. He's not the sort of person I ever saw myself with."

"And what does that mean?"

"I don't know. You know how he made that wood carving in my room?"

"Yes."

"I took it to Marty Carlson."

Gamma quirks an eyebrow. "Whatever for?"

"Just to see," I say with a shrug. "I thought, if he likes it, Riley might be convinced he has options other than playing football."

Gamma folds her arms and purses her lips. "Did he give you permission?"

"I want to surprise him," I say.

She sighs. "Some people would say that being a star player at a top-ranked school is pretty impressive."

"I know, it is," I say, propping my chin in my hand. "He works so hard. If he plays well this season, he could go to the NFL."

"Honey. Why does that make you so miserable?"

"Can you see me dating an NFL player?" I say, gesturing at myself. "I'm not exactly trophy wife material."

Gamma rears up like a rattler. "You are as beautiful as any woman on this earth, and twice as stylish."

"That is clearly not true," I say, laughing. "Beyoncé exists."

Gamma ignores me. "Are you into this man?"

I shrug, not sure how to answer.

"What is stopping you from being into this man?"

"He's a football player," I say, standing up to carry our coffee mugs to the sink. I can't sit still.

"So?"

"So," I say, slamming the cups on the counter. "So, Natalie."

"What about her?"

I bury my face in my hands. "She would hate me."

Gamma comes up behind me and lays her hand on my back. "Lilah. Natalie loved you like a sister. Do you think she would want you to mourn forever?"

I turn to face my grandmother, leaning on the counter. "There's a difference between moving on and flat-out betrayal."

Gamma nods, her eyes far away for a moment. "This Riley—did he have something to do with that?"

"No. He would never." In the short time I've known him, I'm sure of that.

"Then there's only one thing that matters here, Lilah. Does he make you happy?"

"Yes," I blurt. "He's—he makes me feel …. But isn't

that worse? That he should make me so happy when Natalie died in misery?"

My grandmother huffs. "I swear, if Natalie were here I'd cuff her upside the head."

I gape at her, tears standing in my eyes. "You couldn't."

"I could, and I would. What happened to that girl wasn't her fault, but letting it destroy her was. She didn't live long enough to see those monsters in prison, or to help other girls who were assaulted. She let them win," Gamma says fiercely, "and left you behind to try and make sense of things. That's not fair."

"She was hurting, and I didn't do enough to help her," I say, stunned. "She was lost."

"And what are you supposed to do when you're lost? You're supposed to stay where you are and call for help," my grandmother says decisively. She smiles sadly and softly touches my cheek. "Sweet child, I know all about regret, about wondering how you could have done things differently. I still can't sleep sometimes thinking about how I could have done things differently with your mother. But if you let it, it'll eat away at the core of you. And it sure seems to me like you are letting regret get between you and Riley."

I study her face for a long moment. We share the same eyes, the same hair, the same chin. Someday, I hope I'm as wise as she is. "I don't know if I can."

"Then that'll be your choice," she says. She walks back to the table and picks up the sketch of Riley. "Football is part of his life. If you're going to be in his life, you're going to have to accept it."

CHAPTER SEVENTEEN
Lilah

MY HEART IS POUNDING AS I ride my bike to the high-tech practice facility, and not just with the effort of pedaling. I can't believe that I'm here, that I'm doing this.

Riley has mentioned, more than once, that today is something called the Blue and Silver game. It's a Mustang tradition that includes a huge fundraiser for university donors and a showcase workout followed by a laid-back scrimmage that pits first-string offense against second-string defense and vice versa. According to Riley, it's usually something of a party, but I can tell he's worried. After the loss to Hawaii, he's nervous the Blue and Silver game won't do much to prove to potential donors the Mustangs are a team worth investing in.

I may not care about football, but I care how he feels. And though I'm nervous as hell to be showing up to a football event, if it'll help Riley, I'm here.

And then I literally am here. The brand new practice facility looms before me, all steels pillars and high-reflective windows. I bite down annoyance that so much money is dumped on sports when other professors have to practically beg for supplies and updated technology. It cost well over a million dollars to build, and I can't help thinking about all the students who didn't get scholarships, the art and science programs that weren't supported, so that MSU could build this monstrosity.

Not now, Lilah, I admonish myself. Gamma is right. Riley has done all the reaching so far in our relationship, all the compromising. I can't keep asking him to deny this part of himself. It's my turn to make a change.

My newfound determination to embrace football is challenged almost immediately by a guard.

"Miss?" He holds out an arm to stop me at the door. "I'm going to need to see your credentials."

Credentials? This isn't the White House. I chew on my lip before I realize I probably still have my teaching badge somewhere in my bag. Here I am, trying to make a romantic gesture, stymied by security. "Um … one second," I stall, fishing a hand through the slurry of pencils and lipstick tubes at the bottom of my bag. Finally, I tug out my badge and hand it over, trying not to look guilty.

The guard scrutinizes it for a moment, his face hard as stone. "Miss, this isn't sufficient."

I'm about to argue when someone jogs up behind me, calling my name.

It's Reggie, and he's grinning ear to ear. "She's with me. Aren't you, Lilah?" says Reggie. He flashes a winning smile at the security guard. "Had to run out to my car to grab my lucky cleats."

The guard's face transforms when he sees Reggie. He goes from pit bull to puppy in a heartbeat. I have to restrain myself from rolling my eyes.

"Lilah here is from the art department," Reggie says knowingly. "She's here to study the human body in motion. Isn't that right?"

"Uh, yeah," I say, glancing at Reggie. Why is he helping me?

The guard opens the door for us, and Reggie ushers me through to a grand atrium. I stop dead in the middle of the entryway, stunned by the display of wealth around me. Marble floors, brass statues, deep leather seating, and half a dozen TVs showing historic MSU games. "This is where you guys practice?"

"It's not much, but it's home," Reggie quips. "There's facilities here for all the major campus sports, which means close to a thousand students use this building to practice year round."

A thousand sounds like a lot, until you compare it to MSU's entire student body. "Which means there are thirty thousand other students who never step foot in here," I point out, failing to keep the acid out of my tone.

"True," Reggie says, leading me deeper into the facility. "But how much do those students raise in donations every year? How much attention do they get from the alumni?"

"If they had the opportunity—"

"Where do you think those opportunities come from?" Reggie says, opening a heavy door. "The answer is—right here."

The indoor field is bigger and brighter than I'd ever imagined, and right now it's echoing with talk and laughter. There are people everywhere. Men wearing tailored suits chatting with men wearing sweats. Photographers and reporters are scattered around the field, keeping their eyes out for something interesting. And then there are the football players. There has to be at least a hundred of them, all wearing huge pads and blunt helmets and MSU jerseys.

I have a weird moment of dislocation. There's me, with my mohawk and tattoos, wearing a sheer blue dress with a cream bodysuit beneath, in a room with all these clean-cut sports fans. What am I *doing* here?

Reggie points. "Riley's over there."

I follow Reggie's finger, and although he's wearing a helmet and pads, I recognize Riley instantly. Something about his long legs, his strong forearms. He's running a drill that involves running patterns around a large pad. "I don't want to see your feet cross over," a man yells. "Shuffle, shuffle, shuffle!"

Riley runs out of the pattern as another player runs in, and I can see from his high knees and quick feet that he isn't even close to tired yet. I know the exact moment he sees me. His chest lifts in surprise, and I feel a twin lift in me. Pleasure sparkles inside of me as my lips turn up into a smile. And I knew in that moment—*that's* why I'm here. To feed the spark between me and Riley and see if it can grow.

"Ha! I thought so," says Reggie, cuffing me lightly on the shoulder as if I were one of the guys.

"What?"

"I knew you were here to see Riley. The two of you were eying each other through every class."

"We were not," I reply weakly. "We're just …," I trail off, suddenly unable to speak. Riley has whispered to another player and is now jogging over. His uniform accentuates everything I love about his body—shoulders and thighs and arms all on display. "We were totally professional until ...."

"Until ...." Reggie pushes back his dreadlocks and grins. "Hey, whatever you two get up to doesn't matter to me. All I know is, he's been in a way better mood lately and an absolute beast on the field."

Suddenly, I find myself liking Reggie more than ever before. "He has?"

Reggie just grins again. "I'll see you later," he says cheerfully, taking off just as Riley jogs up.

"Hey," he says, surprise and pleasure clear in his voice. "I didn't think I would see you."

In his uniform and helmet, he looks even bigger than usual. "I just wanted to see how everything is going. And, you know, support you." I feel almost shy, showing up on his turf like this.

His smile is clear, even behind his face mask. "Thank you," he says sincerely. "I'm glad you're here."

He reaches out and runs one hand down my arm. Just that simple touch is enough to make heat rush through me. It's probably some sort of arousal poisoning that makes me ask, "Can I stay and watch for a while?"

It doesn't seem possible, but his grin gets even wider. "Sure. There's a spot over there where you can sit." He's pointing to a few rows of bleachers on the sidelines where everyone is either wearing a uniform —football or cheerleading—or an MSU polo shirt. Whatever bravado I had left is fading fast, but one look at Riley's eager face, and I know there's no turning back.

I nod, becoming conscious that there are people watching us and no doubt wondering who Lotto Brulotte is talking to. "You should probably get back to it," I say.

"Probably," he says, tossing a glance over his shoulder. He looks like he wants to touch me again, instead jogs back a few steps, closer to the training field and the dozens of photographers and coaches watching us. He catches my eyes one last time before turning around. "Thank you for coming."

The power of that look makes my knees watery as I walk over to the bleachers. I find a place to perch at the edge—easier to make a quick getaway if this all gets to be too much—and try to look like I belong here. But peering around, it's so obvious that I don't.

Off to my side, a bunch of men and women in blue-and-silver cheer uniforms are taking turns doing back flips. Nearby, there are older men—obviously donors—standing close by. I don't miss the way a few of them elbow each other as one cheerleader tosses another up into the air and she kicks her legs out. She lands, only to be thrown up again, five other girls joining her in a series of stunts that make my head spin. I can handle myself on a bike and run in heels, but what they're doing is close to miraculous.

After a few minutes and polite clapping from the assembled donors, the cheerleaders disperse. A few of them come sit near me in the stands, and it's only a matter of seconds before one girl slides over to me. She takes a long swig of a water bottle then points at my shoes. "Those shoes are killing me."

I tip up one of my black leather boots with diamond-shaped cut-outs. "Thanks." It comes out more as a question than I mean it to.

"My roommate, Lou, would probably try and buy them off your feet. Watch out." She points to a young woman wearing a structural gray dress and some amazing heels standing with a bunch of guys in team apparel. One of the middle-aged guys looks suspiciously like Denzel Washington, and I can't help but think of Gamma and smile.

Next to me, the girl holds out a hand. Her brown skin is a shade lighter than mine, and her hair is relaxed—something I gave up years ago. "I'm Nara, and you're new here, right?" She smiles. "Are you a reporter? My dad's an editor, and I can spot that observer look anywhere."

Lord, am I really that obviously out of place? "I'm a painter, not a reporter," I offer. I chew on the inside of my cheek for a moment before I add, "To be honest, I'm not really sure what I'm looking at."

"Oh!" Nara lights up and slides closer. "Well, then let me fill you in." Her heart-shaped face and wide, mischievous eyes look like they belong on a fairy. I start sketching her as such in my mind.

"So, you've got your offense and your defense," she says, pointing to different groups on the field. "And then your special teams. They started out earlier running drills—sprints, tires, fast feet, the usual—and now they are working on specific skills. In a little bit they'll scrimmage, which is what everyone is waiting to see."

"How can you keep them straight?" I say, looking out over the sea of players.

"You get to know their numbers and positions."

I frown. It takes a minute to find Riley and read the number off his jersey—32. It seems like something I ought to know. To make up for it, I latch onto something I *do* think I've figured out. "And that's Coach Prescott?" I ask, pointing to the Denzel look-alike.

Nara nods and glances over at the tall head coach. He's got dark skin and close-cropped, salt-and-pepper hair, and he seems to be watching the whole field simultaneously. "That's our fearless leader and Lou's doting father."

Ah. Now that I'm looking for it, I can see the resemblance between the two. I'm about to ask more—it's nice having my own, in-person Googlewhen another girl stomps up the bleachers and collapses next to Nara.

"God, football players can be such pains in the ass," the girl says. She's wearing khaki pants and a polo shirt embroidered with the rearing blue mustang. "I had to stitch up Mayhew, and he acted like *he* was doing *me* a favor."

"Are all the rumors true?" Nara asks, craning her neck until she apparently spots him. "He's really as arrogant as they say?"

The girl groans. "Worse." Then she notices me, and her face goes blank. "I mean, he's crazy fast and a huge asset to the team."

Nara laughs and glances at me. "She's not a reporter."

The girl slumps over. "Oh, thank God." She reaches across Nara to extend a hand. "Megan Noble," she says, introducing herself.

"Lilah Stone," I say, shaking her hand. "Are you on the medical staff?"

"God, I wish," she snorts, pushing her reddish ponytail back over her shoulder. "I'm in the physical therapy program, and working with the team is part of our grade. I'm years away from *actually* working here."

"Gotcha." I'm starting to enjoy myself. It occurs to

Head in the Game

me that I haven't had nearly enough girl-time since Natalie died. "And who is this arrogant guy?"

"Sir Benjamin Mayhew-Fancypants," Megan says in a syrupy British accent. "He's a new recruit this year. I guess he played rugby or something and comes from royalty or something. No idea how he ended up here in Colorado. Either way, he's a dick."

"Which is a real burden for every available girl, because he's hot and British and seriously, did I mention hot?" Nara adds, deadpan.

Megan smirks, then focuses on something on the field. "Does Reggie Davis look like he's limping to you?"

I find Reggie on the field, and it does kind of look like he's favoring one foot. "Maybe?"

Megan sighs. "I should go mention it to Garrett. Nice meeting you, Lilah," she says, before taking off again.

Coach Prescott blows his whistle three times, which seems to be the signal for the players to do a fast lap around the field. When Riley passes, he waves at me, and I feel the thrill of it like electricity in my body. I wave back, knowing that heat is flooding my face and I'm wearing a silly grin.

"Riley Brulotte," Nara says. "Nice."

"Yeah," I say dreamily. "It is."

Throughout the scrimmage, when Nara's not cheering, she makes sure to sit with me and explain what's going on. I've never seen the game this close up, and the roughness of it is kind of shocking. And sure, I'm biased and I don't know anything about football, but it seems to me that Riley keeps coming out on top. He's so fast, so strong, so ferocious on the field.

To be honest, it's turning me on.

The game starts winding down when I get a text from Gamma: *I'm going over to Mrs. Levy's house for bridge and gossip. Don't wait up.*

An idea bursts into my head. "Is there anywhere around here I can get a jersey?"

Nara frowns for a second. "Sure," she says. "Plenty of places."

"Good," I say, shooting a quick text to Riley to come to my place when practice is over. "I think it's time I bought one."

CHAPTER EIGHTEEN
Riley

By the time the scrimmage is over, I'm so tired I can barely pull my jersey over my head. It's always supposed to be a laid-back showcase to entertain the donors and get them to pull out the checkbooks, but Coach Prescott seems to have misunderstood the definition of "laid back."

"Christ, he worked us hard today," I grumble, wiping a towel over my face.

"I need it," says Weston miserably as he collapses onto the bench beside me. He's stripped to the waist with an ice pack strapped to his arm. "I wish I could just quit, but there's no one else."

"You'll get there," I say, but privately I have my doubts. West put in a performance riddled with mistakes and second-guesses. He does okay in practice, but it's a different story when anyone is watching. It's frustrating, being able to see all this potential on our team and still not being able to deliver when it matters. This scrimmage was his chance to show the press and alumni that he has what it takes. That he's not going to choke like he did at the disaster that was the National Championship last year. And he's blown it.

Last year during the Blue and Silver game, Jeremy Hudson was throwing long bombs so beautiful they would have made Elway weep. He was one of the best quarterbacks in college ball, and would have been a shoe-in for the NFL if he hadn't been a rapist.

Well, let's be honest ... if he hadn't been caught red-handed.

"Coach believes in you," I say, giving West an encouraging slap on the back. "We all do."

West just shakes his head while I head for the showers. I wish I could be more comforting, but I've got my own problems.

The first conference game is tomorrow. There are only eleven more regular-season games this year, followed by the playoffs ... if we we're lucky. If we we're good. Eleven games that will determine the rest of my life.

The tradition of the Blue and Silver game has always been fun for me, a chance to show off what we can do without the pressure of a real game. But this year, I'd been nervous all day. The air felt like it was swirling with speculation and rumors. If we don't win tomorrow, the rest of the games this season won't matter. We won't get to the playoffs with two losses on our record, hell, we might not even get a good Bowl game at this rate. Even worse, it'll give credence to the loudest rumor of all—that the Mustangs are nothing without MoFo.

Seeing Lilah at practice has been the bright spot in an otherwise-stressful day. I can't believe she came. She's been very clear about her disdain for football. The last week or so, she's been making noises about what a shame it is that football takes up so much of my time, time that I could be using to explore my artistic talent. She doesn't get that carving is something I do to relax. Honestly, I still can't believe that something like what I carved for my final project came out of me. It seems easier right now to pretend it didn't.

It's stressful enough to think about my future without trying to figure how Lilah fits into it. Lilah won't be happy in my small hometown, where the only place to buy clothes is Walmart. If I make the NFL, I can't choose where I go, and I can't see her leaving her grandmother to follow me to an uncertain future.

But maybe, her coming to practice today was a sign that she's willing to budge a little. When I first caught sight of her, she looked so lost, so out-of-place, and so damned beautiful. But then, after just a few minutes, she was laughing with one of the cheerleaders. It gives me hope that, even if she isn't thrilled about it, she can come to terms with this side of me.

I'm glad she's invited me over. I could use a relaxing evening with her and her Gamma. It reminds me of quiet nights at home with my own family. And maybe I'll have the chance to get Lilah alone, steal a few kisses. It's enough just to spend time with her, talk to her, bump her knee under the table where her grandmother can't see.

I don't know where my future is going. But I do know I want to find a way to keep her in my life.

My phone rings just as I pull into her driveway. I groan when I see that it's my dad calling. He's been driving me crazy, calling and emailing at least twice a day. He's more nervous about the season than I am.

I'm not in the mood to talk to him, but he will just keep calling if I don't answer.

"Hey, Dad."

"How'd it go today?" he asks, without even a greeting.

"Good," I say, forcing cheer into my voice.

"Just good? How is that Sawyer kid throwing?"

I hesitate, which tells my father everything. "Shit. Riley, I'm worried that we made the wrong choice about staying at MSU. I wish I could be there to see what's really going on."

"Yeah, but you're not," I say, my voice sharper than I intended. "I'm here. This is my life, my future."

"Yeah, but we're a team, son. I want to see you succeed."

I suck in a breath. "You want to see me succeed in football."

"Of course."

"You don't care about anything else."

"That's not true," Dad says.

"Yes, it is. You never ask me about my classes or my friends. All you care about is that I make the NFL, so I can live out your dreams."

I've never said this to my dad before, but if feels like such a relief to finally say it. To clear it out of my chest.

"Riley—"

"Look, I'm sick of it! Sick of your expectations. What happens if I fail, dad? What happens then?"

I don't wait for an answer, just click the phone off. My dad calls back almost immediately, but I send it to voicemail. I can't take any more pressure tonight. All I want is to see my girl and let tomorrow take care of itself.

I take a deep breath as I approach the house, trying to calm the frustration bubbling inside me. Lilah texted me that she left the door unlocked and that I should come right in.

"Lilah?" I call into the dark rooms.

"Back here," she calls. I follow the light coming from her bedroom and the faint tinkling of music. The rest of the house is dark and silent, and it hits me that maybe Gamma isn't here. But who knows—everything feels so mixed up right now. I'm already feeling bad about hanging up on my dad, and I should really call him back after I've settled down.

Then I turn into Lilah's room, and every thought drains out of my head.

She's lying in her bed, which would have been enough by itself to get my dick hard. We've had sex standing, sitting, braced against a wall, inside, outside, and in the back of my truck ... but never in an honest-to-goodness bed. She's curled against soft pillows in a pool of golden light, and she looks so gorgeous she almost isn't real.

But that isn't all. She was wearing a Mustangs jersey. *My* Mustangs jersey, with my number on the front. I'm not an egotistical guy, but seeing her curvy body tucked inside *my* jersey has a primal pleasure rising inside me.

Mine.

"Hi, Riley," she says, her voice sultry. She trails one hand up her bare leg, her red fingernails contrasting with the umber of her skin. Her lips are red too, sleek and pouty, and she has done something to her eyes to make them bigger and sleepier. She's left her hair natural, thick and curly, and I can't wait to get my hands in it.

"Hi," I breathe, trying to take her in all at once. "You look incredible."

She licks her lips and smiles. "I figured, with the big game tomorrow, you might need a little extra encouragement."

I nod, still feeling dumb. "Your grandma's not here?"

Lilah shakes her head, then scoots over a bit on the bed to make room for me.

I nearly trip trying to kick off my shoes and strip off my pants at the same time. I toss a couple of condoms on the dresser, grinning when Lilah raises her eyebrows. "I'm going to need a lot of encouragement," I say, pulling my shirt over my head and dropping it on the floor. She reaches out for me as I walk naked toward the bed. Mentally, I take a photo of that moment—my woman, welcoming me.

I sigh as I settle in against her. My cock is already rock hard, but all I want for the moment is to be close to her. She is so soft, so warm. Underneath the desire, there is bone-deep comfort that comes from simply being in her arms.

She's wearing some musky scent that teases my senses, drawing my nose to her neck and throat. She laughs as I nuzzle into her and throws her leg over mine, trying to draw me closer. "My bed's not very big."

"But it's a bed," I say, stretching luxuriously. My feet are hanging off the end, but I'm used to that. "I finally got you in a bed."

She bites her lip and looks away from me. "I'm sorry that I don't feel comfortable in your dorm. We could have been in a bed all along, but—"

"Hey. You don't need to apologize for anything." I stroke my hand over her cheek, marveling at the softness of her skin. "But you should come over sometime. If nothing else, you can check out my collection of carvings."

She presses her lips together and nods. "I can do that. I'm sorry that I've been so stubborn about it. It's just, with Natalie ...." She shakes her head, frowning. "It felt disrespectful to her, somehow. But that's just foolish. If I want to be in your life, I should see how you live."

I nudge her with my forehead, wanting to see her smile again. "So you want to be part of my life?"

She nods, something like a plea in her eyes.

"That's what I want too," I say, my voice thick. "I want you in every part of my life."

I kiss her as her lips start to turn up. It's slow, languorous. We're savoring each other. I run my hands over the surface of the jersey, molding the curves of her body.

She purrs with pleasure and runs her hands over me in turn. Her lips leave mine and trail down my chin, my throat, sending shivers down my spine. "Lilah," I whisper, for the simple pleasure of saying her name.

She pushes at me until I lay on my back, and she kneels beside me. It gives her hands the freedom to run over my chest and shoulders while her mouth kisses hot trails over my chest. I moan when she tweaks my nipple between her fingers, then gasp when she takes the other with her teeth. My hips thrust up involuntarily, desperate for attention. "You're killing me," I manage to gasp.

She lifts her mouth from my chest and kisses me

again, deep and dirty. At the same time, she strokes her hand down the center of my abs and takes my cock in her grip. I gasp into her mouth as she begins to stroke the whole length of me, rubbing the head with her thumb.

"Oh, baby," I groan, letting my legs fall open. "That feels so good."

"I can do better," she purrs, resettling herself between my legs. Keeping her eyes on mine, she takes my cock between her bright red lips.

"Fuck, Lilah. You're always beautiful, but you look so gorgeous with my cock in your mouth."

I can see from the way her eyes fly to mine that she's shocked, but that she's also turned on. Her ass is in the air now as she leans down to work on me with her mouth and hands. She knows exactly how to keep me on the edge, speeding up and slowing down until I'm desperate to come.

As if she can hear my thoughts, she rises up until she's sitting on her knees. She pulls off the jersey, revealing that she's gloriously naked but for a pair of cotton MSU panties.

I stroke her ass, tracing the team logo. "Baby. For me?"

"For you," she confirms, turning so I can admire the way they cut high on her ass.

I pull her down next to me and roll on top so our positions are reversed. It's my turn to run my hands all over body, to use my mouth on her hard nipples. She's squirming and moaning by the time I peel off those soaked panties and position myself between her legs, rolling a condom into place.

I take a second to appreciate the way she looks, sprawled out against the rumpled sheets. Her breasts

Head in the Game

heaving, her eyes glittering with desire. I take my cock in hand and rub the tip of it against her clit, making her moan and cry. She's so slick, so ready. And still I tease her, driving her desperate body, until she clutches at my shoulders and begs me to fuck her.

When I finally sink into her, it's as if there's no world beyond this bed. No breath beyond the breath we share. Her eyes flutter open, her pupils wide and focused on my face. In that moment, all her defenses are down. I can see into her, see the love inside me reflected in her.

It's so much, too much, so I kiss her. That just makes the feeling spiral out and radiate through my entire body. I'm pumping inside her, driving us both closer to madness, and yet my heart feels like it's swelling to the breaking point. Her kiss is like a gift, like she's giving some part of herself to me in a way she hasn't before. Something in me breaks open to her, something that will never be whole again without her.

She tears her mouth from mine to cry out. I bury my face in her neck and follow.

CHAPTER NINETEEN
Lilah

My double bed has never been this crowded, but I wouldn't change it for the world. Riley makes up for taking up the vast majority of my bed by holding me as close as possible. He has a sleepy smile on his face, his eyes closed, his hair mussed. Love hits me like a fist in the chest.

There's no going back now. I've been falling for a long time—probably since that first day of class, when he pissed me off so much. I should have known then that my reaction to him was more than the usual.

Now, here we are, tangled up in the bed where I've never brought a man. I spent money to please him that should have been in my savings account. I went to a football game, for God's sake. I'm definitely in deep. I lay my hand over his chest so I can feel the strong, steady beat of his heart.

Normally, this would be the part where I freak out. I've had previous relationships that I had to end because they got too real. There aren't a lot of people who have been in my life for the long term. My

Gamma. Natalie, until she died. But no guys. I've always felt like there was no point investing in a relationship that would inevitably end.

But this thing with Riley ... for the first time in my life, I'm really willing to make it work. My grandmother was right, he's worth compromising for. He has already changed my life by making me rethink how much I hate football players. I know now that I blamed the whole team for something only a few of them did. And I believe Riley when he says the team culture has changed. It feels good to let go of my anger. It makes me realize that Natalie wouldn't have wanted me to carry it in the first place.

For most of my life, I've avoided opening up to people. I pour all my emotions into my art to keep myself from saying them out loud. But I'm ready to do things differently. Riley is a wonderful man. He won't hurt me, he won't leave me. Look at how hard I've tried to push him away! Now I'm ready to pull him in, hold on tight. I'm ready to open my heart to him, my life, my everything.

"What happened to the carving?"

Oh, it was just too perfect. I got an email from Marty earlier in the evening while I was waiting for Riley, and I couldn't wait to share my news. Well, I could wait a little while. Now Riley can see how much faith I have in him, how I'm willing to work on his behalf.

"That's the next surprise," I say, snuggling him closer. "I was offered five grand for your piece."

He pushes me back so he can see my face. "What?"

"I took your piece to the Melee Gallery, where I sell most of my work. Marty Carlson—he's the guy who normally teaches the art class—he flipped over the piece. He said he'd buy it from me on the spot."

"Five grand? Five thousand dollars?"

"Isn't that great?" I ask, wiggling with glee. "I mean, I knew you were good. But if you can command this sort of price now, think of how much you'll be able to make when you're established. Marty said that if you had enough work, he'd build a whole show around you!"

Where I expected him to whoop with joy, his face darkens. "You sold it?"

"No, Riley, I'm proving to you that you can make money as an artist. You don't have to play football!"

This last part probably comes out a little too pleased. Riley's serious brown eyes go molten with anger. "Jesus, are we still on this? When are you going to get over this? Every other girl I've dated loved that I was a football player."

"I'm not like every girl," I say, resenting the comparison but trying to keep my temper in check. "If you want to play football, that's fine, but—"

"Fine?" he scoffs, putting space between our naked bodies. "Do you have any idea how hard I'm working? How much this matters to me?"

"If course I know," I say, desperate to get back on solid ground. "I just wanted you to know that you have options. You talk about it like it's the NFL or nothing, but it doesn't have to be that way."

He laughs, but there's no humor in it. "Tell that to my father."

I don't know what to say. "Can't you see," I try tentatively, "this is an alternative. You could have a different kind of life."

His gaze, which had been fixed on the empty bookshelf where his piece had been, returns to mine.

"Your kind of life?"

"Yes," I whisper.

"Digging up your feelings so you can sell them?"

"That's not what I do," I say, though part of me wonders if it isn't the truth. "Besides, what I do with my work is my business."

"Yeah, right. But business has been shitty, hasn't it? You told me yourself. I bet that five grand helped, huh? How much do you think you'll get from the little figurines upstairs?"

How can he believe that I would sell anything he's given me? The thought makes me sick. "It was an offer. I didn't take it. Marty asked if he could keep it overnight and take some pictures."

"You didn't sell it."

"No."

He exhales hard. "And you're not going to?"

"Not unless you decide you want to. But Riley, like I said—you could make some real money. You could have a career."

"Because the career I have now isn't good enough?"

"Riley," I say, my voice breaking as he rolls out of bed and starts dressing. "I didn't mean it like that."

"Seriously, Lilah. Do you have any idea how many girls would kill to be with a football player?" He punches his arms through the sleeves of his shirt.

"Is that what Jeremy Hudson used to say?" I instantly regret the low blow, but I'm angry now too. Why isn't he listening to me?

Riley's shoulders stiffen with shock. "Right, I forgot. Because we're all rapists, we're all monsters. We're all exactly the same."

"That's not—"

"Look, I'm tired of the explanations, the excuses.

You'd do anything to get me away from football. Why can't you understand how much it means to me?"

I hug my arms around my naked body. Only minutes ago, we'd been close and warm. Now he feels like he's across an unbridgeable gulf. "I don't want to lose you. I can get over it. I'm *getting* over it."

"If you weren't so stubborn in the first place, there wouldn't even be a problem."

I am stubborn, and I don't consider it a flaw. "You don't get to tell me how to live my life."

"Oh, but you get to tell me how to live mine? Everything is on your terms, in your space, in your time. I feel like I'm being pulled in a thousand directions, and it's killing me." He shakes his head, turning away from me. "I thought you were different. I thought you saw me, really saw me."

"I do, Riley." I follow him out of bed, naked and vulnerable. Taking a chance, I lay my hand on his tense back. "I see you."

He shakes me off. My heart falls as quickly as my hand. "Please, Riley. I wasn't trying to hurt you."

He turns to me, and the pain in his eyes lances me. "You're just another person who wants to tell me what to do with my life. You can't accept me as I am. And I'm starting to wonder if you ever will."

The world tilts on its axis as he walks out the door. I call out to him, my voice cracking on his name. But the only answer is the slam of the front door.

After Riley leaves, I sink to the floor with my arms wrapped tightly around myself. Hot tears are spilling from my eyes even as my skin prickles with cold, but I can't think of anything but the searing pain inside me. My mind feels shattered, every thought causing a new wound. How did it all go so wrong?

This is why I've always been careful with my emotions. Loving someone is like spinning a web between two souls. You may be stronger together, but it doesn't take much to shred the connections. That's how I feel inside—shredded, laid open, lost. Riley. I hurt Riley, and he hurt me.

A single thought pierces through the pain. *This* is how I know I'm in love with him. My heart is crying out to him, begging for him to come back so we can hurt each other some more.

I can hear the empty house echoing around me. If I were to call my grandmother, she would come home to comfort me. But I don't want to talk to her; I don't want to confess how badly I fucked things up. How badly I always fuck things up. Hiccuping, I tip over onto my side, pulling the blanket from the bed to wrap around my shoulders.

I didn't meant to hurt him. But I assumed that he would be as thrilled as I was with the idea of living as an artist. I deliberately ignored the things he said about how much football means to him because I didn't want it to be true. He was clear that he wasn't interested in making money off of his art. Just because I don't understand it doesn't mean I shouldn't respect it. At the moment, I don't have much respect for myself.

Was he right? Was I selling pieces of my soul away?

I've never liked looking at my own work. I can't help but be critical; I'm not bad, but I can always get better. More than that, it's that looking at my own paintings makes me think of the pieces of myself I scraped off or broke away in order to make the work possible. The thoughts and feelings that fill a landscape with energy, or intensity, or yearning. I let myself feel them, feel every brutal centimeter of those emotions, so I can remove them from myself. Once a painting is done, I want it gone.

But Riley is wrong if he thinks it's inherently wrong to make money off my paintings. Those paintings kept food on our table when Gamma couldn't work and the medical bills were looming. How dare he judge me for that? I want him here, so I can yell at him for it.

I have the stray thought that all my careful makeup is ruined. It might make me feel pathetic and vain, but it's enough to make me get up, pull on a long T-shirt, and go wash my face. When I catch sight of myself in the mirror, I break down again. I can see the bleak sorrow in my own eyes.

I started tonight with such good intentions. I wanted to tell him how impressive he was in the Blue and Silver game; I wanted to tell him that while I still didn't understand the game, I was going to try. For him. And then I would tell him about the offer on his piece. I would tell him how proud I am that he's talented in so many ways.

I would tell him how much I love him.

For the first time, I can understand why Natalie didn't call me for help before she committed suicide. How can you admit to another person that the darkness has taken over? How do you get through this kind of pain without part of you dying inside?

Maybe that's why I haven't been able to paint since Natalie died. Since Natalie committed suicide. Why don't I use that term? "Died" makes it sound like something happened to her, instead of something she chose. That's the part that I can't get past, can't get over. Natalie *chose* to die. She joined the ranks of people I loved, who chose to leave me.

Riley.

Natalie.

My mother.

I've spent my whole life trying to pretend that not having a mother doesn't matter to me. I have Gamma, and that's enough—more than enough. But there's always been this shard inside me. My own mother didn't want me, has never wanted me. That thought has been festering inside me for most of my life, poisoning everything. It's made me terrified of how easily I could lose everything.

Gamma has never failed me. She gave me every bit of her love, attention, and wisdom. She has never let me doubt that she loves me and that she expects me to be the best version of myself. But with her heart problems, I could lose her anytime. For the last three years, since her heart attack, I've been terrified that the river of life is going to take her away. It kept me from going to art school, it kept me from experimenting with my art. Loving her so much has stunted my growth, and I'm afraid it's permanent.

For so much of my life, there was Natalie. We were so close, it was as if we shared the same mind. She supported my decision not to go to art school because it meant that I would stay in Granite with her while she was going to MSU. She never wanted to leave this town, and I pretended to feel the same. Going to New York to accept the Pitkin last year was one of the few times we'd been apart, and it was terrifying and glorious to be on my own. But then I came back and found that rape had crumpled Natalie up, tore her apart. I couldn't put her back together again.

And now there was Riley. Since I met him, all the parts of myself I've shut down, shut off, have come rushing back to life. He's nothing like I thought he would be, and goddammit, why is that so hard for me to accept? Nothing is ever going be what I think it will be. All my plans and dreams and expectations and fears are ripping me apart. I'm trying to make him into someone else, which is crazy. He's so wonderful, exactly as he is.

I wash my face, the cold water shocking me awake. It's still early, but I have no interest in the dinner I'd planned to eat with Riley. Maybe later, when my stomach isn't a bath of acid. Sleep seems impossible. Instead, I do the thing I always do when the pain is too terrible to bear. I slip on some yoga pants, pull back my hair, and I go to my studio to paint.

My eyes are too raw to handle the lights, so I let the moonlight guide me up the stairs. My bare feet barely disturb the silence of the house. In my studio, I'm greeted by the dozens of blank canvases perched against the wall. I dig through them until I find a small one. Then, sitting on my stool with a palette full of oils, I begin to paint.

I don't do portraits. I paint landscapes, because it's always been easier for me to translate what I feel into rocks and mountains rather than human faces. But I need to understand something that I've never let myself feel before. I need to look myself in the eye, and see who I really am.

I work from the mirror in my studio, not letting myself think about what my hands are doing. I'm tempted to give myself some of the flair I would normally have—artfully styled hair, smoothed features, a fabulous outfit. Instead, I paint myself as I am, in this moment.

Rounded shoulders under a ragged shirt. Toes curled over the bars of my stool, clenched tight. Aching, tired eyes. Frown lines burrowing into my skin where my smile used to show. And I make myself feel it, make myself feel all the things I normally ignore. I lower myself in the bleeding chasm of my loneliness, and force myself to wallow there.

When I finish, the sun is peeking over the horizon. My eyes have dried long ago, and I feel hollowed out. My muscles are sore—it has been months since I've painted this way. Carefully, I wash my brushes and palette and set them to dry. Then I turn to look at myself.

I tamp down my urge to focus on the technical details. Instead, I make myself look at the girl in the painting as if she were a stranger.

The first thing I think is that her sharp chin reminds me of my grandmother. Sweet and stubborn. The tilt of her head makes it look like she's listening to something, trying to hear an explanation that's too distant to understand. Her eyes are haunted, heartbroken ... and determined.

I thought I was out of tears, but fresh ones jump to my eyes. In the eyes of the girl in the painting, I can see the strength I don't feel. The girl in the painting isn't going to let her own mistakes ruin her life. In the bleakness of her eyes—*my* eyes—I can see a glimmer of confidence that refuses to be extinguished.

If I could talk to my mother, I would tell her that Gamma and I don't need her. If I could talk to Natalie, I would tell her that she will always be my best friend and that I wish she had let me help her get better.

Both of them are beyond me. But Riley ... Riley isn't gone. And I'm not going to let him out of my life without telling him how much he means to me.

CHAPTER TWENTY
Riley

THERE ARE FEWER GUYS HOLDING tight to my carved figurines in the locker room today. Reggie is still thumbing the miniature version of his lucky shoes. A lot of good that will do him.

Ben is doing high-knees and jumping jacks right here in the middle of the locker room, taking up all the available space and air with his energy.

"Hey, man, can you cool it and relax for a minute." I want some peace and quiet for a second, and the flurry of motion in front of my eyes is making me dizzy. I'm trying to find a way to block out the noise. All the noise of the reporters and television shows questioning our capabilities. The speculation about whether we'll win a single game, if we lost to Hawaii. And the buzzing is only getting louder with every thump of Ben's shoes against the concrete.

"I'm just limbering up, mate. You can't go out on the field cold."

This is a pretty stupid statement considering we have never gone into a game without a pre-game warm up. No team in the history of sports has gone into a game without coaches taking everyone through a warm-up. Ben extends his arms and starts twisting his torso from side to side, throwing his arms out over the rest of us, just expecting us to get out of the way. It's all I can do to stay seated on the bench. Reggie is giving him the eyes of death, but I don't have the energy to quell whatever fight is about to start.

Just then, Coach Prescott strides in, and everyone shuts up and takes a seat. Even Ben. Coach starts talking, which is better than everyone's chatter and Ben's frantic stretching. The talking is easier to tune out. I'm not in the mood for some phony pep talk. Nothing he can say will magically make us better players. I stare at the floor and wait for it to be time. Time to trudge onto the field. Time to get this over with.

We shuffle out of the locker room, and we're jogging because we have to, but there's no buoyancy in our step. My hand reaches up automatically to slap our team slogan—"Can't Stop the Stampede"—and I realize with a pang that we didn't come together for the chant before we left the locker room. How could we have all forgotten? Are there so few of us veterans that it's not an engrained tradition anymore? Can a tradition that seemed so deep and permanent just vanish like that? The realization sits uneasy on my shoulders.

The stands are splattered with big chunks of red and white. If you restrict yourself to looking only at the one side of the field, it'd be hard to tell who's turf we're on. The Utes have feathers in their hair, and they're jeering us as we jog out onto the field. I try to focus on blue and gold. This is our home advantage, we're not going to be intimidated just because some University of Utah fans decided they wanted to spend their weekend in a car.

The energy is off right from the start. The fans aren't as boisterous as they were last game. All of their fears from last year's National Championship game, all of the off-season wondering and speculating about whether or not we're going to be any good this year ... it's all but been answered. With a single game, the student body, the town, the whole state have given up on us. Even my own dad doesn't believe in us.

We punt the ball off to Utah and I sit on the sidelines, with the edge of a finger in my mouth, nervously chewing my nail. A red jersey waves his hand in the air for a fair catch. At least they won't run it back for a touchdown.

Utah runs the ball, eeking it forward and not risking a turnover. They only pick up a few yards at a time, but it's good enough to earn them a first down. It's safe, but boring to watch, and I can feel the air being sucked from the stadium. The slow march down the field continues, making it back it to the forty yard line before our defense holds them and they're forced to kick. They try for a field goal, but the ball takes a bad bounce off the post, and we get the ball back unscathed.

I huddle up with the rest of the offense, and we look to Prescott for the play.

"All right boys, it's 0-0. We got a chance to get ahead here. Let's show them who we are. Blue Oyster."

I look to West. His face is white, and I don't blame him. It's a ballsy play. It has Ben shooting down the field like a rocket and West throwing the longest spiral that we have in the playbook. If we pull it off, we'll have a jolt of confidence and energy. If we don't ... I don't know. I guess Prescott figures we have the next down to make it up. I hope to God he knows what he's doing. I ignore my dad's voice creeping into my brain trying to convince me that Prescott is the doom of us all.

I jog out onto the field, my cleats digging into the turf I know so well. But this all feels so ... off. I'm used to fans screaming in the stands, of the sort of energy that makes me feel like a god. Instead, now every step onto the field—surrounded by thousands of eyes judging us, watching for us to *fail*—it's like a biting wind that makes me want to hang my head. I fight past the feeling and jut my chin out. I can't give up. I *won't* give up.

We line up, and I block out everything else—the jeers from the Utes, the pressure from the fans, everything. I have to be here, in this moment, ready to play this game with everything I have left.

Reggie snaps the ball back to West. I hit my defender hard and keep the block. West rolls back, giving himself space, and then he lets the ball go. It flies through the air in a perfect arc and I can already tell that it and Ben are on the same trajectory. If he catches the ball, no one will be able to stop him. For all his arrogance and bluster, he is one of the fastest wide receivers I've ever witnessed. This might actually work. It might actually ....

A red shirt is tight on Ben, and just as he's about to pull away, hands grip his shirt, holding him back enough so that the ball just slips through his fingers. A whistle blows.

"Holding. Number 59 on the defense. Ten yard

penalty," the referee announces. All around us, boos and cheers butt up against each other. But I focus on one thing: West got the ball off. He didn't hesitate. It steels my spine, if only a little.

After that, Coach plays it a little safer. West throws a shovel pass off to a newbie running back, Shane Crews, but Crews chickens out from running it up the center like the play calls for. He tries to take it outside, but runs out of field and ends up out of bounds with a one-yard gain.

"Fuck!" I shout, stalking back to the line for the next play.

I take a deep breath. I'm over-thinking every play. *The play's over, Lotto. Move on to the next one.*

Except the next one called makes my stomach flip. This one is all me. If the play goes south, I'll have no one to blame but myself.

It all happens so fast. There's the snap, and then I'm bolting up the field, running as fast as my legs can take me. I feel the blood pumping through me, my muscles straining and bunching. I push off my defender, and as I'm turning to cut back and catch the ball, I slip on the field. I take a wrong step and feel my balance falter. I catch myself, but too late. The ball bounces off my hands and into the air. I reach my arms out for it, to recover the ball and save the catch, but my defender is back on me and he wants the ball as badly as I do. I dive forward and feel the lung-busting press of two-hundred pounds of muscle as the Ute lands on top of me. The ball falls just out of reach and dies. Incomplete.

By the time the clock winds down to halftime, I'm drenched with sweat and my muscles are burning. The whole team looks like we've just been through a week of bootcamp, and the game is only half over. We've managed to keep the score close, Utah's up 7-3. It's not the shellacking we got from Hawaii, but it feels just as disastrous. We're making the same mistakes we made then, and there's no sign things will improve.

Technically, anyone could win it, but I'm just not sure we have anything left in us.

CHAPTER TWENTY-ONE
Riley

WE DRAG OURSELVES DOWN THE tunnel toward the locker room. I have never felt this way before as a Mustang. Sure, we've lost games before, but it's never felt this hopeless.

Even Reggie looks deflated. And West ... West looks miserable.

We pile into the locker room, shoulder pads bumping, helmets dangling from our hands. Dimly, I can hear the cheery music of the marching band playing fight songs on the field. At least the spectators will get some entertainment. I've felt the weight of their opinions the whole first half. If we lose this game, what will become of the Mustangs?

"Have a seat, boys," Coach Prescott says, stalking back and forth at the front of the locker room. Most of the team collapses onto the rows of benches, but I lean against the wall. I'm afraid that if I sit, I'll never get up again.

"Well," Coach says, pulling off his hat and running his hands through his hair. "That was a great first half."

A murmur of depressed laughter huffs through the room. "Great" isn't exactly the word I'd use.

Coach scrubs his hands over his face, looking at us. "Gentlemen, I'm proud of you."

I shift my shoulders uncomfortably. Proud?

"Yes, proud," Coach says, answering my unasked question. "When we started working together, I saw a bunch of boys with raw talent, and some skill, but no heart. We're all here for different reasons. Some of you have scholarships, some of you transferred from other programs ... some of you have never even played football before. But here's the thing we have in common," Coach says, his voice rough with emotion. "We all are here because we want a chance. A chance to make a change. To be part of a team. To prove that we are more than what people think we are."

Some guys are picking up their heads, the glimmer of determination sparkling in their eyes. Coach continues. "We all made a choice to be on this team, and ride out this season. It was always going to be rocky. It was always going to be rough. I didn't have to apply for this job. Oh, no, I could be cozy back at my old school, running a winning football program. Do you know why I applied for this job? Do you?"

A couple of guys shake their heads.

"I applied for this job because of *you*. Because I wanted to work with the kind of young men who would take big chances. And in that way, you have made me proud."

Ben Mayhew glares at Coach Prescott defiantly, as if refusing to be inspired. "A fat lot of good that will do us," he says bitterly. "We're still going to lose."

"I'm speaking, young man," Coach says, so calmly and coldly that Ben lowers his head. "But I want y'all to listen to him. Because he's not wrong. That's what people will be saying out there in the stadium right now. That's what the sportscasters are going to be saying tomorrow. They're going to say that this team was gutted by scandal, and that every single one of you are pale imitations of what the team used to be."

The room is silent as Coach lets that sink in.

"But that's not what I see," he says, his voice rising in tenor. "I see young men who are willing to work hard and surprise everyone—including themselves. I see men who have spent the last few weeks learning the most important lesson you can learn: That if you play like you're alone out there, you will be. You'll lose."

Coach pauses, and I feel alone. I really do.

"But here's the flip side of that. When we work together, when we play as a team, we can be better than we are alone. Stronger. Faster. Smarter. Hawkins, did you pass the ball to Reed when you were being tackled?"

"No," Hawkins says sullenly. "I didn't want to lose possession."

"Are you kidding me, man?" Reed says. "I was right there, I was holding out my hands to you."

Coach points at Reed. "That's what I'm saying. I'm going to ask y'all to do something for me, and I wouldn't ask if I didn't think you could do it. You all took a chance on yourselves when you became a Mustang. Now take a chance on each other. I know it feels like a risk," he says, holding up his hands. "But what do you have to lose?"

I can't help but think about Lilah. I haven't given her a chance to explain. I haven't given myself a chance to think about the offer, and what selling my carvings might mean. Why have I shut down all my chances, trying to convince myself that I have none?

"I want you to go out there," Coach says, "and play this second half like your lives depend on it. Because they do. I'm not talking about winning or losing or any of that. I'm saying that if you can go out there and believe in each other, we've already won."

With that, Coach strides out of the locker room. He stops just at the entrance, where West is hovering, and says something to our quarterback that makes him breathe deep and stand up straight.

For a moment, we all sit there, not sure how to react. Then Reggie stands up and says, "Can't stop."

No one replies. Reggie looks over the team and says again, firmly, "Can't stop."

"Won't stop," I reply, and Reggie breaks into a grin.

"Can't stop," Reggie says, stomping on the floor. "Won't stop. Don't stop."

A few other guys take up the chant. Then everyone is on their feet, faces pale and determined. "Can't stop, won't stop, don't stop. Can't stop, won't stop, don't stop. Can't stop, won't stop, don't stop."

Reggie jumps up on a bench. "What're they trying to stop?"

"The Stampede!"

"Who's gonna stop us?"

"Nobody!"

"Who are we?" Reggie bellows.

"Mustangs!" We shout back.

"Who are we?" Reggie shouts even louder, beating his chest.

"Mustangs!"

"Can't stop the stampede!"

On cue, all the guys start running in place and

slapping the walls, the benches, the lockers. The cacophony is incredible. Reggie stands in the center of it all, basking in the energy we are making together. I can feel it too, the swirling currents of possibility. But at the center of all that possibility, I feel a stone weight trying to drag me down.

What am I doing here? How did I get here? Is this even where I want to be?

One of the assistant coaches taps me on the shoulder. "Riley. Your dad is on the phone."

"My dad?" The sinking feeling turns to fear. He knows phones are off-limits during a game. So if he called anyway .... "Is everything okay?"

I follow the assistant coach into a small office, where a phone is resting off the hook. "We're going back out in three minutes," he says, before closing the door behind me.

"Dad?"

"Riley," my father says, relief clear in his voice.

"Is everyone okay? Did something happen—"

"Everyone's fine. I had to talk to you, and I know you don't want to talk to me right now, but Riley, I'm watching this game, and I just feel sick inside."

"I know, Dad," I say, collapsing against the cinderblock wall. "I'm fucking up."

"That's not it. Riley, it breaks my heart thinking that you don't know how much I love you."

The sick ball of failure in my stomach stills. "What?"

"I love you, son, no matter what. I don't care if you make the NFL. Hell, I'd love to have you back home to work with me on the farm. Or whatever you want. You are my greatest accomplishment, exactly as you are."

My heart thumps hard in my chest as tears prick

my eyes. "Dad."

"Let me finish. I pushed you toward football because it seemed like a chance at a great life, but if that's not what you want, son, that's fine. I will be proud of you, no matter what. I'm always proud of you."

"Dad," I say thickly. "This isn't exactly getting me pumped to go back onto the field."

He laughs, but I can hear from the wavering in his voice that he's near tears as well. "Don't worry about who's watching or what they're going to think. Just get out there and have fun with it."

I look out into the locker room, where the stampede has devolved into a bunch of guys laughing and wrestling. "The coach said we needed to take a chance on each other."

"I agree with him. The talent is there, Riley. What you do with it is up to you."

I take a deep breath. "Thanks, Dad. I love you too. Thanks for calling, thanks for … everything."

I set down the handset, feeling part of my bleak mood lift. My father has always rooted for me, always been my biggest fan. We've been talking about the NFL for so long, I guess we both assumed that was the ultimate goal. But I need to stop thinking about the NFL. I can't control the future. The only thing I can control is what I do, right here, in this moment.

And what I'm going to do is join the stampede.

We emerge out of the locker room and into the tunnel with our spirits high and our energy burning. We're only one touchdown from pulling ahead. We can do this.

There are the usual VIPs and fans in the tunnel, all

dressed in Mustangs gear. My gaze skims over one avid fan, then wrenches back. Was that ... Lilah?

I do a double take, still jogging with the team. Then I use one of the moves Coach Prescott taught me, jigging out of line and ducking back before the assistant coach can see me.

Sure enough, it *is* her. Or is it? This woman is wearing my jersey with a pair of tight jeans painted with the Mustangs logo. The same logo is on her cheek, along with my number. Her mohawk is tied with blue and silver ribbons, and there are three earrings dangling from each ear—an M, an S, and a U.

I wrenched off my helmet to see her better. "I feel like this is some weird fantasy."

"It feels weird to me too." Under the perfect makeup and the wild hair, her eyes are serious and worried. "But I plan on getting used to it."

Something painful moves inside me. "I said terrible things to you last night," I start.

"No, let me go first," she says, laying a hand on my chest. I can't feel the pressure through my pads, but I feel it just the same. "I have so much more to apologize for. Riley, I never should have tried to change you. From the very beginning, you've been honest about who you are, and you should be proud of everything you've accomplished. I let the past screw my head up, and I blamed you for things that were never your fault. Please forgive me."

"Done," I say immediately. Her shocked gaze shoots to mine. "I do love surprising you."

"Well, wait until I'm finished. Because I'm not going to apologize for taking your piece to Marty. I would never sell it without your permission, and I'll never do anything like that again, but I wanted you to know:

You're talented, Riley. And not just at knocking people down. I needed you to know, whatever happens, that you have so much more potential than I can imagine."

The ache settles deeper, touching deep inside me. "Lilah—"

"Brulotte. What are you doing?"

I look up to see Coach, his hat pulled low over his eyes. The tunnel is nearly empty as the teams spill out on the field for the second half. "I need one minute," I say, already knowing it isn't enough.

"You get out there right now or you'll have the rest of the season to chat up pretty women." He nods at Lilah, then adds before he walks away, "I like your hair."

Lilah tilts her head to the side, showing off the designs etched into the thatch of her scalp. Two rearing Mustangs. I bark out a laugh. The ache inside me is blooming into something warmer, deeper, sweeter than I'd ever imagined. I grab Lilah's hand, pulling her with me out on to the field.

CHAPTER TWENTY-TWO
Lilah

"Come with me," Riley says, his grin boyish and irresistible.

"Where are—Riley! I'm not allowed out there!"

Riley doesn't stop dragging me down the tunnel, out onto the field. "You're going to love it."

I want to protest, but I'm hit by a wall of sound unlike anything I've ever experienced. I've never even been to a real football game, let alone been on the field. My eyes pop trying to take in everything at once.

The field is greener than I'd expected, the lines whiter. Everywhere I look, there are faces—fans rising up all around me like I'm at the bottom of a canyon. The sidelines are teeming with people, all carrying clipboards and wearing headsets and acting very official. "Riley," I say timidly, "where can I stand where I won't fuck anything up?"

He pulls me in for a quick kiss and scans the crowd. Just then, one of the girls I'd met the other day—Megan, I think—runs up to me. "Lilah, what are you doing here?"

"She's with me," Riley says, squeezing me tight.

"Well, I could use an extra set of hands. Do you mind if I borrow her?"

"No problem," Riley says, then turns to me. "I'm so happy you're here."

My heart turns over in my chest. "I love you," I say fast, trying to get used to saying it.

Riley's beaming smile melts my heart. "I love you, too."

I turn to Megan, still brimming with happiness, only to be confronted with her raised eyebrow. "Can you see past all those hearts in your eyes?"

"Probably."

"Good. My asshole boss wants me to move all of the stretchers for absolutely no reason, and I could use a hand."

"Sure, I'll help," I say. Then the crowd roars as the team takes the field.

I pick out Riley from his number, taking his position on the field. "What are they doing?"

"Getting ready to snap the ball."

When I looked at her blankly, she lowers her eyebrows. "How much do you know about this game?"

"Basically nothing."

"And you're with Lotto?" Another time, her skepticism might have offended me, but not today. I'm too happy.

"Yes," I say proudly. "Yes, I am."

Megan studies me, then sighs. "Well, I guess now is the time to learn."

The students around me start screaming "blue" in unison, drawing the word out until it's less a color and more a primal chant. Across the stadium, I watch in awe as others "silver." Megan belts out a "blue" of her own, the annoyance in her eyes from earlier replaced with elation. Next time the chant circles back to us, I throw my shoulders back, take a deep breath and bellow out a loud "blue!"

I guess this is part of being a football fan. I can get used to this.

Megan has to walk me through the second half, giving me play by plays the whole way. I barely understand it, but I come away with a tiny bit more respect for players, because these rules are confusing.

The energy around me is infectious, and even though I can't really figure out all the rules, I'm sitting on the edge of my seat. Riley catches a ball, and my heart soars. I leap up like every other fan and scream my head off, so proud to see his strong legs propel him down the field. He holds his arm out straight and manages to keep one of the bad guys in red from tackling him, but there's another fucker after him. I'm screaming myself hoarse by now as the red jersey blasts into Riley, and my heart stops as he hits the ground. It's not until he gets up that I let out my breath and realize that my hand is clung tightly around Megan's wrist.

She pats my hand.

"He's tough," she says.

I nod. She's telling the truth, but there's still a knot in my stomach from seeing him laid out on the ground.

I look up at the clock, and I can't believe there are only two minutes left in the game. The score is 14-10, and the Utes are still up. I came here ready to be a good girlfriend, and I can't imagine that I'll sit home and watch football games for the fun of it, but when my man is on the field, I can't help but be riveted to the action.

We're only down by 4, we can do this. The thought jumps into my mind before I can censor myself. *We.* I am now with the Mustangs enough that my brain is thinking in "we"s.

Weston Sawyer has the ball and he's looking around in that lost puppy dog way he's been looking all game.

"I swear, if he would just throw the goddamn ball," I mutter to myself, but Megan finishes the sentence for me.

"We'd have twice the yardage." Her hand flies to her mouth. "It's not my place to be critical."

I laugh out loud. No one else seems to mind gossiping about the Mustangs.

"Throw it to Lotto!" I yell. It's the first time I've acknowledged Riley's silly football nickname, but I kind of like the way it feels coming out of my mouth.

To my surprise, West does throw it to Riley—a long, arching throw that looks like it's going to land too far in front of him. But Riley somehow sprints even faster and catches the ball practically in stride. He runs off the side of the field before the red-shirted giants have a chance to hit him.

"Out of bounds," Megan explains. "We keep the ball."

On the next play, West passes the ball off to him again, and Riley uses his bulk and his strength to barrel his way through two red shirts who try to knock him down. He takes a hit on his right side that sends him into the field. My fists clench, but he gets up quickly this time. He brushes off his pants, but the bright green grass stains don't budge. I can't wait to take them off of him and give him a hot bath. I want to have his naked body wrapped around me while I massage all his muscles.

"We're in the redzone now," Megan says at my side, pulling me out of my mini-fantasy.

"That's good?"

Riley keeps killing it out there. He's shining like a star, so much brighter than everyone else on the field. It's no wonder West keeps giving the ball to him. He's absolutely on fire. And after every play, he smiles back at *me*.

"Yeah, it's good. It means we're inside the twenty-yard line. Only twenty yards between us and touchdown."

I look back up at the clock. There's less than a minute left.

The Utes have caught on to West always giving the ball to Riley, and they're all over him. West stammers, looking for someone else to give the ball to, but runs out of time. He gets hit hard by a red jersey. Luckily, he still has the ball in his arms when he goes down.

There's thirty seconds left, and I just can't sit anymore. I want the Mustangs to win more than I thought possible. Utah is gunning for Riley again, but Reggie comes out of nowhere and blocks a defender, letting Riley get away. West lets go of the ball, and I can see Riley lock onto it. He runs the short distance away from the cluster of players and catches the ball. It lands in his arms, and he cradles it— almost gently—as he turns toward the end zone. He faces a defender, but steps with his right foot, and spins with his back to the defender. The defender lunges forward, but Riley's past him, his momentum moving ever closer to a touchdown. Riley is so close now, his arms are stretching forward with the football, his upper body leaning toward victory.

The defender hits him hard in the side and Riley juts forward as he falls. His body stretches, until each and every seventy-two inches of him is reaching for the goal as his body slams into the ground.

The tip of the ball looks like it's just barely touching the end zone.

The entire stadium goes quiet. I realize I'm holding Megan's arm again, tightly, but she's completely frozen too.

The referee lifts his arms straight over head and fifty-thousand fans in the stadium jump to their feet and completely lose their minds. I'm right there with them. There are still ten seconds left on the clock, but it doesn't seem to matter. The whole team is rushing the field, and Megan grabs my arm, making sure I'm running out there, too.

I only need that little nudge of encouragement, and then I know exactly where I'm going. I run straight to Riley, pride bursting in my chest.

When I reach him, Riley lifts me in his arms, as he's done so many times. But for the first time, I let myself really feel the joy of it, the freedom. I feel the knowledge that this man will always lift me up, never hold me down. There is triumphant music blaring through the air, shouts and cheers and swarms of celebrating people. There's so much joy inside me, all around me, that it spills out of me in laughter and tears.

"Come home with me," Riley says—more, shouts—over the crowd. He yanks his helmet off and drops it to the field. "I want you to meet my family."

I nod. "I will. After the season is over."

"You don't have to come to all my games," Riley starts, but I stop him with a shake of my head.

"Try and stop me. Though I should probably buy a seat next time. I'll bring Gamma, she'll love it. Maybe I can even introduce her to Coach Denzel."

Riley's face creases with worry. "Lilah, I don't know what the future holds. I could be living anywhere in the country next year."

I take his face in my hands. "So could I."

"What do you mean?"

"I want to go to art school." Saying it feels like a dam has broken inside me. "I told myself I didn't care, but I do. I loved teaching you, and all the other students in that class. I want to be in that environment, I want to push myself in new directions. Gamma is so much healthier, she can manage without me. Marty will still sell my paintings, if they're any good, and if he can't, then who cares? I'll figure it out."

"What are you saying?"

"I'm saying, if you get drafted, I'll follow you. And if you don't, you can follow me."

The furrow between Riley's brows lifts. He lays a hand on my cheek, his eyes deep and hopeful. "I love you so much, Lilah."

"I love you too," I say, the words flooding out of my mouth. "Oh, Riley. I love you too."

He pulls me into his arms, an oasis amid the madness. His pads are hard and thick, making him even more huge than usual, and I can't help thinking that this big, strong, wonderful man belongs to me. When Riley kisses me, that joy multiplies and expands. I want this moment to last forever. And I will make sure it does—I will paint it for Riley, paint us together in this moment. Not to sell—just for us. Because there will be losses, there will be bad times, there will be tragedy.

But together, Riley and I can face all those things. So long as neither one of us ever forgets this one perfect moment.

Printed in Great Britain
by Amazon